SIX YEARS' WORTH

A Novel Written by:

Daniel Lance Wright

Special thanks to Steve Sanders for the cover design.
The author, Daniel Lance Wright, can be contacted at:

dannylwright@txwi.net

First printing, December 2006
© August, 2004 Daniel Lance Wright

ISBN 13: 978-0-9779407-4-5

Father's Press, LLC
Lee's Summit, MO (816) 554-2156
E-Mail: fatherspress@yahoo.com
www.fatherspress.com
www.mikesmitley.com

Thanks Ang
You're a pal

Danny Stright

"Only some of us can learn from other people's experiences; the rest of us have to be the other people." (Old Farmer's Almanac)

Most of us have glimpsed at least one of that segment of society without homes, hope or happiness. The stories are varied and numerous as the stars in the sky. But one cannot help but wonder: What brought them to such a point of despair? What paradigm sets a person on any given path? Is it environmental, psychological or simply a conscious choice? At what point, in a person's life, does it become devalued? Is it something from birth, a traumatic childhood, or a major catastrophe in adulthood?

It is a complex issue with many questions, and, as many answers.

This story is dedicated to all people who find themselves feeling alone, forgotten or discarded.

Compassion is the ever-present companion of understanding.

ONE

Pulling his tattered wallet from a hip pocket, he then cleaned his other pockets out as well. That wallet and a few coins was all the money he had—thirty seven dollars. He placed the contents on the rickety apple crate that served as a nightstand. He then pulled out a pocketknife and a bottle of sleeping pills to lay with it. Next to the small bottle, he placed a pint of cheap gin. Both containers had dirty labels, soiled beyond legibility from months of handling, yet neither had ever been opened, the seal on the gin bottle remained unbroken.

He pushed back onto the bed. He leaned against the wall and pulled his knees to his chest. Perching his stubbly bearded chin on his folded arms and, like every other night, he considered his options. The lure of that gin bottle was attractive; its proximity to the sleeping pills presented the ultimate answer, in combination. Together, they were his friends, constant companions and a treasured means to an end, should he ever choose it. It was the only thing in his life he felt was absolute. He trusted that. He thought about eternal peace, free from scorn and free from hurting. He didn't need chemicals to become intoxicated by that thought. It was an incredible sense of freedom to simply contemplate death, to *know* there was that option.

They called him Pop. How he ended up in a small town in the heart of farming country is still a matter of conjecture. Possibly, it was a simple matter of where he had been when running was no longer an option. It seemed reasonable. He stepped off a freight train in Green Meadow, Texas, stopped at the elevator at the edge of town to load cars with new crop grain. Green Meadow is the county seat of Bentley County, located on a vast plain of endless cotton farms in the northern portion of the state. The curve of the earth was the only thing obstructing the view around Green Meadow, or so the joke went. He'd overheard it just the day before, twice. The landscape was a patchwork of fields in various shades of green and brown. Seen from a vantage point high in the sky, it would surely appear as an intricately detailed patchwork quilt spread over the earth.

This day had been typically hot and dry, no real difference from any August day, except the cumulus clouds joined forces in ever-increasing numbers, billowing skyward. Near day's end they pulled together and towered, creating a lone summer thunderstorm.

Pop watched the rain and knew its size would cheat someone as it dropped all its moisture on a few thirsty and very lucky farms, hardly moving at all, falling in a sudden torrent just before sunset, like squeezing a saturated sponge onto the parched earth. Rain, in any form, would surely be welcomed, although brief and confined to a small area. The edges of the rain shafts told the tale, adjoining farms would tally different amounts of rain by year's end. *I wonder if God has favorites? Some are blessed while most are not. Something as simple as rain, life-giving moisture, yet most will only know thirst.* He drew a deep breath. Exhalation was slow and laced with despair. As the rain diminished, so did the light of day. Darkness quickly veiled the small town's deserted streets.

Pop shoved off the edge of the small iron bed and shuffled to the open window of his dingy second-story walkup. His thinning hair did a slow dance across his lined forehead. Looking and feeling older than his sixty-two years, he stared across Main Street. A red and blue-white neon sign flashed below him, over the entrance to the jewelry store. It cast an eerie glow across his worn face.

Music from a distant radio in an open window drifted his way on the muggy nocturnal breeze, compounding the old man's apprehension, guilt and loneliness that seemed bottomless. But there were no tears, all had been cried out long ago.

The tattered clothing he wore had not been changed since stowing away on a southbound freight train in Chicago six days ago. Little better than rags, the garments bore the marks

2

and foul odor of battle—the daily struggle to survive. When he boarded the train, his only goal was to get away from Chicago and as far south as possible. Otherwise, he didn't care where. Another brutal winter was forecast for the Midwest. He wanted no more of them.

The darkened street below still held remnants of that brief thunderstorm and glistened with reflected light from lamps lining the sidewalk. The air was heavy with moisture that simply could not stay long on pavement that retained heat from a scorching late summer day. Far in the distance, he heard the sound of a truck changing gears, a grinding transmission followed by uneven acceleration. The quiet of this rural community allowed even the most distant sounds to carry for miles.

Pop shifted his feet and stumbled; forced, at last, to pay attention to fatigue. Utter exhaustion ground him down. For reasons he would not be able to explain, he didn't want to sleep, ever. He always wanted to squeeze as much out of each day as possible, yet his lifestyle contradicted that. Even to him, it was a puzzle. But, he assumed it was fear of falling asleep and never waking and left it at that. Desire and his aching body were at odds again. Whether he chose to sleep or not, he soon would be. His eyes became heavy. The lids could no longer bear their weight. More dragging his feet than stepping, he walked back to the small and rusting bed against the wall. He sat down hard. The springs groaned under his weight. Exhaustion ruled. He wilted over and dozed. The rain-cooled breeze caressed him, pulling him under. Crushing fatigue pressed him into a deep, dreamless sleep. The mournful call of a whippoorwill in a distant cotton field fell on ears that did not hear. Paul Odell Peterson, somehow, managed to survive one more day.

**

Boom! Pop rolled from his bed, falling to the floor with a thud. He covered his head, an involuntary response to an unknown threat. Heart pounding, he lay still, expecting to hear screams and shrieks of terror. Instead, he heard children—laughing children.

Reluctantly, his protective grip loosened on his head, to better hear, to better understand what might be happening.

The lone window in the dilapidated apartment faced east, yet sunlight did not stream in, as it should in the morning, the sun had already made its way to a position much higher in the sky. From shortly after dark the night before, until late this morning, he slept without movement or any conscious thought. Now, groggy and uncertain, he had to piece together his location and a reason for being here. Once these things fell into place, he breathed easier, struggling to stand on sleep-weakened legs, with the added soreness of strains brought on by a hectic week of traveling by rail—a trip that offered nights of cold metal or wooden floors to sleep on and no cover. Dragging his feet, he walked to the window, overlooking the small downtown area and took in sights and sounds of a bustling community.

Boom! An old dump truck loaded with part of some farmer's grain crop backfired again on its way to the elevator at the edge of town. His fear had had no relevance—though curiosity was suddenly aroused.

He descended the open stairwell, ending at the sidewalk between the jewelry store and a hardware store. Two doors down he saw a small diner. It had been nearly two days since his last meal. He knew he needed food soon. All else must wait. He began walking and noticed the odd looks he received along the sidewalk. *Even a well-dressed stranger would have a problem with acceptance. If this town is like most small towns, it's a tight-knit society. The way I look must scare them.* Pop was far from well dressed, groomed or even clean. He saw some of them steal glances then smile, but it appeared more nervous tic than sincere, like they'd been caught looking and a smile. was the excuse. He knew without asking, the townspeople were not deliberately unfriendly, but strangers had to be viewed as potential threats to property and safety,

4

especially if their presence could not be accounted for quickly. By his own experience, trust was not something lavished but earned, one good deed at a time. This north Texas community was surely no different.

When Pop entered the diner, the general buzz of conversation trailed off. People stared. He paused and surveyed the crowd, but it was cursory, and only for a second, before claiming a swivel stool at the end of the counter, as far away from the nearest customer as possible. Their opinion of him was of no concern, but he instinctively avoided potential problems. An elderly woman approached him from the other side of the counter.

"I sure could use a menu and a cup of coffee, ma'am," he said then smiled nervously, glancing up in bursts.

She held a towel to her nose. The smell of his unbathed body was pungent and clearly nauseating. "I'm sorry, Sir, but I can't serve you and respectfully request you leave…immediately." She fanned the towel between them.

A fleeting expression of shock left his face. "Could I at least have a cup of coffee to go?" He had given up so much in life, resigning to that situation was just one more affirmation of a life not worth fighting for, possibly not worth living.

A burly man dressed in white pants and a t-shirt, belly lopping over his belt and tattoos dotting his arms, stepped out of the kitchen when he heard the woman's comment and joined her behind the counter, likely the woman's spouse. His silent presence was an unmistakable show of support. Neither made an effort to comply with Pop's request.

Pop hung his head, defeated, trying to decide what to do next. His hesitation was brief, as he slid backwards from the stool.

In a booth across the diner, a portly middle-aged man in a cowboy hat sat with his wife and small son eating an early lunch. Shaking his head with deep-set sympathetic eyes and a saddened brow, he watched the confrontation but made no effort to intervene, supporting their decision to oust the old man.

"Who is that man, Daddy?" The youngster asked, confused.

"Son," his father said, pushing his hat back with the tip of his finger, "that man is probably just a hobo that came into town on the train that runs down by the grain elevator."

"What's a hobo, Daddy?"

He sighed. "Well, they're people who choose not to settle in one area or have a career. They just wander from town to town."

"But why would anyone want to live like that?"

"I don't know son," his father said, patience thinning, "there could be a thousand reasons...all different." He resumed eating, putting an end to the rapid-fire questions.

Still uncertain what his next move should be, Pop left the diner. On aching legs he stopped at the stairwell leading up to his room. Sitting down slowly was not an option. He dropped heavily onto the lower step, groaning softly, as the hard wooden step met his rear end. A sharp, yet brief, pain subsided.

Thinking on the situation, no solutions came to him, in fact all thoughts jumbled, having no beginning and no end, his eyes empty and staring. People walking by did not—would not, return his look or acknowledged his presence. He was invisible. The first thought he locked on to were his friends, the pill bottle and the gin bottle. They beckoned. It was a way out. At the moment, the allure was more inviting than it had been in the past. He took comfort in it, and considered blissfully sliding into a thoughtless, worry-free abyss. He felt his face relax, a smile trying to take hold.

He shook away the thought and the smile, neither given a chance to settle in. Once more, for some inexplicable reason, he banished the notion. This time more readily than usual. *Maybe it's the fresh, clean air. It's nice to smell air without diesel fumes.* He brushed the long fine strands of hair from his face and studied his disintegrating shoes then draped his arms over his knees.

"Mister?"

Pop looked up, directly into the eyes of a small boy holding a Styrofoam cup out to him.

"Here, Mister. It's the coffee you wanted." The youngster insisted by shoving the cup directly under his nose, steam escaping the small hole in its cap.

Pop leaned away, studying this brash little man long and hard without expression. He looked the youngster over then head to toe but all he could see was a big heart and innocence. "What's your name, boy?" he finally asked.

"Colt. Daddy said they named me that because I'm such a pistol."

"Do your momma and daddy know where you are?" he asked, taking the cup from the lad, aware for one brief moment, a smile, a *real* smile, tugged at his lips.

"Oh, yes, Sir," the youngster said, "Daddy gave me fifty cents to buy the coffee."

Pop took a long, slow sip. He closed his eyes and savored the taste. When he again opened them, he pulled his gaze back down to the boy in front of him. "How old are you, Colt?"

"I'm five," he said with a gleam, holding up a hand, all fingers spread wide. "But I'll be six real soon," he said, as a blurted afterthought. "I'll be in the first grade." Shoving his fists into his pockets, he grinned wide, his mouth disappeared into shining pudgy cheeks, as he stood proud and straight.

Pop fidgeted, not knowing what to say. The act of kindness was beginning to feel more like a confrontation. He became uncomfortable. "Run on back to the diner boy," he said, suddenly feeling awkward. "Your momma and daddy will wonder what happened to you."

Colt spun and marched like a miniature soldier. He had taken only a few steps when Pop called to him. "Thanks, Colt. Thanks for the coffee."

TWO

The old pickup truck bounced and swayed, as Tom and Marge Bradshaw ambled down the long straight section-line dirt road toward home. Green Meadow, shrinking in the rearview mirror, ultimately disappeared in a cloud of dust behind the old truck. At a period in Texas history when homesteading was still the norm, farm and ranch land was platted in six-hundred-forty acre blocks, or sections, outlined by access ways that became known as section-line roads, which were hardly ever paved and could extend for miles.

Marge brushed loose hair clippings from Colt's forehead, attempting to smooth the errant part of his fresh haircut. She saw by his darting eyes and antsy behavior that his mind worked overtime. "Did giving that poor old man a cup of coffee make you feel better?" she asked. A large and loving woman, Marge continued combing the boy's hair with her fingertips. Her own hair was pulled into a tight bun accentuating her rosy cheeks and large, caring eyes.

"Yep, sure did," he said and beamed with pride. "But, I still don't understand why someone would want to live like that?"

Marge looked at Tom. No further prompt was necessary. He took the cue.

"Colt, it's a complicated thing that has no easy answer," his father told him. "Shoot! There might *not* be a good answer...just one anyway. It could have been a single terrible thing that happened in his life, or, it might have been a whole string of events, taking years to get to that point, a slow but steady life-long decline. Who knows? Even he might not be able to answer that question for you."

The truck jerked and shimmied, as it ran across a shallow washout in the road. A heated blast of August air streamed through the open truck cab. Tom pushed his hat back and patted his damp forehead with the long sleeve of his shirt.

"Well, if it was just one *bad* thing, wouldn't one *good* thing make it better?" Colt asked. It didn't make sense within the framework of the boy's still-developing basis for right and wrong, why the old man's plight could not be fixed with a few minor adjustments.

Tom laughed at his son's innocence. "You *are* a straight shooter, Colt." Steering the old pickup off to the side of the road, Tom stopped at the mailbox at the end of the driveway to their farm. Choking dust trailing them caught up and engulfed the truck. He extracted the box's contents, and then wheeled on to the unpaved road up to the house. With a clank and a rattle, they drove on to their home, the dust cloud following, as if on a leash. The thunderstorm in Green Meadow the night before had not made it as far north as the Bradshaw farm.

Looking out across the sprawling cotton field, Marge said, "Tom you'll never get that cotton picker down those rows, if you don't get rid of that overgrown Johnson grass and those huge careless weeds the hoe hands missed. Do you realize that?" Her pride was tempered with concern. "I swear. You just can't find good hoe hands anymore."

"Yeah, I know," Tom said then sighed. "But it needs to be hired out. I just don't have time to do it myself." Removing his Stetson, he wiped sweat from his forehead on his sleeve. "But, you're right. It'll choke the machinery and slow the harvest down if I don't do something…and it needs to be done soon."

The Bradshaw's were proud of their farm, not just its ability to produce a fine livelihood but its appearance as well. The long driveway sported neatly cut ditches, lined with tall evergreens, planted decades before, providing a welcoming, shady approach to their home. It also served as a windbreak during brutal spring sandstorms the plains of Texas were noted for. Aside from a few well-placed trees around the house, the countryside was, otherwise, treeless. Beyond the driveway, on both sides, row after row of cotton stalks arced gently in long

10

rows for hundreds of yards, matching the contour of erosion control terraces.

The extended yard around their home had the appearance of a small village; numerous barns, sheds, and other outbuildings surrounded the house, covering over an acre. To an outsider it might seem humorous, but to a Texas farmer it was a serious display of priorities when the barn was larger, newer and more expensive than the house they lived in. The Bradshaw farm lent credibility to folklore. Tom had constructed a massive steel building large enough to store three tractors and implements, plus a large shop area with benches and tools galore, as well as an office walled off in a corner, while the house itself was vintage pink stucco, reminiscent of the mid-fifties, and of modest size.

The old pickup truck creaked to a stop near the house. Marge sighed contentedly at the timeless scene before them, free-roaming chickens scratching the ground, occasionally taking a short flight after a tasty grasshopper, the squeal and grunt of hogs, and the bawl of a calf at its mothers' side.

"Who ya goin' to hire to cut those weeds, Daddy?" Colt asked, as he used all four of his short appendages to climb to the ground from the truck cab.

Tom rubbed his forehead as though it might release a thought. "Humph. I'm not sure," he said. "Most of the traveling crews have moved on. We're getting too close to harvest now. They've probably all gone back to the Rio Grande Valley to pick autumn vegetables." He paused. "But there aren't really that many weeds, just big.

"You think one man could do it, Daddy?"

Tom shrugged. "Sure."

"How about that fella in Green Meadow? You know, the one I gave the coffee to? I bet he could do it. I bet he'd do ya a *great* job."

Tom did not respond. He began unloading groceries and feed sacks from the bed of the pickup, hoping Colt might tire of waiting for an answer and leave him alone. But, Colt stood waiting with uncanny patience for a five-year old, until his father bent to drop a bag of chicken feed. Tom suddenly found

11

himself looking directly into the eyes of his determined son. Squatting on his heals so he could talk to Colt eye to eye, he tipped his hat and said, "I'll make you a deal, little man. I'll go into town tomorrow morning, and if he's still there, I'll ask him. How about that? Make ya happy?"

Colt grinned big and said, "You betcha." He hugged his father and walked off to play.

Tom sat on his haunches and smiled, as his only child walked proudly away. He made the promise, but didn't honestly expect the man to be in Green Meadow when he and Colt returned.

**

Pop had paid fifty dollars to stay a full week in his room and did not have enough for another week. Food was not his only consideration. A decision must be made. The bitterness of winter that he ran from in Chicago could not be ignored in Green Meadow either. *How could such a small town offer much in the way of temporary employment? I think I'd better get back on that train and keep heading south, all the way to the coast...Houston, maybe.*

The thought, once made, began to dog him. It became the focal point of every one thereafter, but he procrastinated. There was something appealing about this place. He couldn't quite put a finger on it. Fascination worked overtime at cracking hardened apathy.

Using more of his precious cash, he bought a loaf of bread, a small package of luncheon meat and sat on a bench on the courthouse square. He ate and considered his options. Eating hungrily, the pangs of an empty stomach eased. As comfort increased, he began to notice things. With each bite, mental clarity improved. It was concrete evidence he had become malnourished and didn't even realize it. Continuing to eat his sandwich, he examined his surroundings. The quaintness and serenity of the setting became the reason for his growing fascination. If he had options to choose from, none came to him, other than leaving town and heading south or staying in Green Meadow and trying to make a life. His disgust with a large metropolitan setting could not overcome the fact that Green Meadow was too small to sustain him through the winter. When his money was gone, he'd be in trouble. That fascination and glimmer of hope began to crumble.

As he took a final bite, save for a small piece of crust, he decided that he had to keep moving south. The notion of staying, he figured, was an idle whim, a wish for better times and nothing more.

Pop knew the train came through town twice a day. The overnight run didn't slow down, but the one that came through about mid-morning stopped at the elevator to unhitch cars on a siding to load grain. Then another engine would come along, hitch up the loaded cars and move on, taking the load to the Port of Houston for export. This was the obvious choice. There really was no other, because it would be stopped long enough to search for a decent boxcar that offered at least a little comfort. Besides, Houston was as far south as he could travel on this line. It would be warmer during the coming winter and there would surely be better chances for panhandling and temporary jobs in a population rich city as that. His mind was set; he would leave the next morning on a southbound train.

Swallowing the last bite, he flicked the remaining crumbs he held toward a gathering flock of sparrows, fighting for the morsel, chirping merrily. Looking with interest, he noticed a few people milling about across the street. A couple of old men debated something, gesturing wildly and laughing. A mother and daughter examined a window display, and a young, unattended boy played with a balsawood glider under the giant oak, elm and pecan trees on the courthouse square. Brilliant blue sky and sunshine was the perfect complement to this Rockwellian slice of Americana.

Envy knotted his gut. And then, deep inside, a spark was struck. A question bubbled up in the old man's mind: *What would happen to me if I chose to stay instead?* He couldn't seem to get his mind back on the plan to leave.

THREE

"There it is Daddy. That's where he lives." Colt stood in the pickup cab, his nose inches from the windshield, pointing at the open stairwell across the street from the courthouse.

The sky was brilliantly clear, but the sun still rose, casting long westerly pointing shadows.

Tom eased the old truck into a diagonal parking space in front of Bickley's Hardware Store. The brakes squealed, as it came to a full stop. Casting a stern eye, "Now Colt, you wait here in the pickup while I go find out about that fella. Ya hear?" Tom hopped out of the truck and looked back at his son, holding the pose of a disciplinarian. He was not moving until he had a promise.

"Yeah. Okay. Sure," Colt said with ample enthusiasm.

Tom noticed Raeford Willis standing in front of his jewelry store enjoying the morning air, wiping smudges from the display windows. "Mornin' Raeford," he said, tipping his hat to a woman passing between them.

"Good morning Tom," he said. "The wife and I drove by your farm Sunday afternoon. Y'all have a really fine lookin' cotton crop. It should be a good Christmas at the Bradshaw's this year." He drew a broad grin. "Maybe you'll be able to afford that diamond pendant Marge has been admiring for so long." He winked.

Aware of the piece of jewelry Raeford referred to, Tom's only response was a noncommittal smile. "Raeford," he said, "who's that man you rented the room over your store to?"

"Can't say for sure. He told me to call him Pop. He'll be leaving later this morning." He refolded his towel and sprayed cleaner on it. "Headin' south toward Houston, I believe he said."

Tom looked to the window just above the sign over the door to Raeford's store and saw no movement. "Is he up there right now?" Tom asked, pointing to the open window.

15

"I think so."

Tom thanked Raeford. He turned back to check on Colt, gesturing for the little guy to be patient. He took the stairs up, two at a time, ending at the door at the top, Pop's place. It was the equivalent of three stories up, but was directly over the high ceiling in the jewelry store. He knocked on the well-worn door, rattling it with every blow. After a few seconds with no answer, the door suddenly flung open with a harsh grating noise against the buckled plank floor.

Tom stepped back, startled. "Are you Pop?"

Pop nodded then stepped forward, looking up at Tom without expression.

Tom had to take another backward step to maintain an odorless buffer. "Would you be interested in temporary farm work?" he asked.

Pop chewed the inside of his cheek. When the silence was about to become uncomfortable, "Who are you and how do you know me?"

"I'm sorry." Tom extended his hand. "I apologize for being so abrupt. My name is Tom Bradshaw and my son Colt—"

"Colt?" The familiarity of the name struck him. He then took Tom's hand and shook it. "Oh, yeah. Colt. The Pistol." The old man's mannerism softened.

"Yeah," Tom said, "That's right. The Pistol."

Because he needed traveling cash and didn't figure a few days delay would make appreciable difference in his plan to head south, Pop accepted Tom's proposition with little haggling.

When they appeared together at the bottom of the stairwell and stepped out onto the sunny sidewalk, Colt leaped from the cab of the pickup and shouted excitedly, "Hello there."

"Hello there to you, too," Pop said. His expression remained neutral, not wanting to appear too obliged, or plant seeds of an eventual emotional entanglement of some kind. The stay would be short. It was best to keep the relationship professional and bland.

Tom was polite, but insisted Pop rode in the bed of the truck. Colt was equally insistent that he rode in the back with his newfound friend. Tom acquiesced.

The morning air was pleasant, as Tom pulled the old truck onto the highway toward home. It would be several hours before the late August heat became uncomfortable. Tom kept the sliding rear window of the pickup cab open. Behind him, Colt besieged the old man with a nonstop barrage of questions that Pop wasn't answering.

"Is Colt your real name?" Pop said, interrupting the youngster's chatter, speaking loud enough to be heard above the wind noise.

"Oh, no, sir. My real name is Rodney Oliver Bradshaw."

With no smile and no inflection, "Humph. I like Colt better."

"Yeah, me too." "Is Pop your real name?"

Pop stared at the boy for a moment and wondered if he'd opened a Pandora's Box with his question about the boy's name, but it was of his doing, so he figured satisfying the youngster's curiosity on it was the price of the answer. "Sort of. It's an acronym."

Screwing up his face, "An acro—what?"

"An acronym. It's a word made from the first letters of other words. My full name is Paul Odell Peterson...P-O-P. See what I mean?"

Colt turned to watch the familiar landmarks roll by. He swayed and bounced with each bump and pothole. The wind whipped his hair. He fixed a stare at Green Meadow getting smaller by the minute. "I like Pop better," he finally said, with a single, decisive nod.

Tom turned onto the driveway when he reached their farm but drove on past the house and rolled up to the big metal barn beyond the backyard of their home. An old hen flew low across the path of the truck, startled. Tom rolled out of the pickup. "Come on Pop, I'll show you where you'll be staying for a few days."

Pop followed him through the massive sliding double doors of the big barn to the small office in the front corner. Tom unlocked a door so rickety that locking it had to have been a formality. It barely fit the jamb. The room was not intended to be living quarters, spartanly furnished with an old sofa in the far corner and a desk and chair at the opposite end near a lavatory and toilet. Tipping his cowboy hat back on his head, Tom put his hands on a waist partially hidden by a belly camouflaging his belt and said, "Well, Pop. This may not be much, but it's about all I have to offer. The nights are cool around here, so sleeping shouldn't be a problem. You won't be in here much during the heat of the day anyway." Waiting for a comment, Tom ran his finger through the dust and cobwebs on the desk, somewhat embarrassed. "You do have running water here, too." He flushed the toilet.

Pop didn't bother to look around. "This'll do."

"I'll have Colt bring you something to eat in a few minutes," Tom said, turning to go out the door. "Afterwards we'll talk about the job."

Pop nodded and watched Tom walk away then moved to the single window across the small room. He brushed aside cobwebs and blew dust off one of the panes. He looked out across the gently rolling terrain that was the Bradshaw farm, becoming lost in the labyrinth of his thoughts, his most faithful companions over the years. Time passed.

Colt reappeared holding a bag out to him. "Here ya go, Pop."

He turned to see the lad holding a bag. "What ya got there, boy?"

Colt dropped the sack on the floor, pulling out neatly folded pants, a shirt and a pair of thick-soled boots. "Momma said it's hard to work if you're not comfortable. So, while we were in town looking for you, she found some of Daddy's clothes he can't wear anymore, just in case you decided to work for us. Not sure you noticed, but my Daddy's stomach is getting pretty darned big."

Pop didn't know how to respond. He took the items and grunted.

Colt reached into the bag again. This time, he pulled out a bar of soap, a towel and a washcloth. "Momma also said she'd be happy to feed you, but she wants you at the table, not out here eatin' with the animals."

"She said that, did she?"

"Yep. That means you got to take a bath."

Colt grinned big.

"A bribe, eh?"

"I guess. What's a bribe?"

Pop shook the fold from the shirt and examined it. "Being paid to do something usually illegal or unpopular."

"Oh, she's not gonna pay you, just feed you."

Pop looked at Colt expressionless at first. Then a faint smile appeared. "The food, boy," he said. "*Food* is the payment." He held up the boots and looked them over, studying their condition.

"Oh. Okay," Colt said. "But if food can be used as money; how do you carry it around? Do they make food wallets?"

Pop snapped a glance at him. This time, the grin was unmistakable, and crooked.

The boy continued staring at Pop with a confused puppy dog look. "Well, when you taste Momma's fried chicken, you'll be glad she bribed you." Having done his duty the boy marched away then stopped suddenly and whirled back. "Oh, yeah. She wanted me to tell you lunch will be ready in thirty minutes, and to knock on the back door when you get to the house. Okie dokie?"

Pop dropped the boots, nodding, "I'll be there." This time he watched the youngster with interest as the little man disappeared through the door. He had no idea what to make of the situation, but he was hungry. He stripped his raggedy clothes and got down to business with the bar of soap, a washcloth and a small basin of water. He did the best he could with the resources he had.

Once he was as clean as he was going to be, he sat in the chair near the desk and split a starched leg of the pants with the point of his toe and repeated the process with the other leg. In

19

an effort to loosen the stiff fabric of his pants and shirt, he bent his knees and rolled his neck. When he had done about all he could do, the old man made one final check in the small mirror above the sink. He ran his fingers through his thin hair, and then slid his palm across his scruffy beard. "Well, Mrs. Bradshaw," he mumbled, "I hope this meets with your approval. It's the best I can do."

It was late morning. The August sun had moved to a point high in the sky. The summer heat created a mirage, distorting distant images, making them appear to be under slow moving water.

Emerging from the barn, he startled a chicken. The fowl's flapping wings blew puffs of dust into the air as it sped away. Its claws barely touched the ground. In no hurry, Pop sauntered along. Fingers laced behind him, he inspected his surroundings.

Aside from the scratching of the chickens, an occasional grunt from nearby pigs and the bawl of calves, there were no familiar sounds he could identify with, accustomed as he was to the constant growls, groans and whines of motorized vehicles, echoing horn honks and a general cacophony of human voices, sounds common to city life. Instead, he heard the buzz of a bee coming from a great distance, passing near him, on to the next flower or blossom. He passed a small machine shed with a welder, grinders and various metal working tools. He strolled on to the low gate of a fence around the backyard of the Bradshaw home. Pushing it open, a large attached spring let out a single note much like a plucked guitar string. He walked beneath a huge, sprawling elm tree that shaded the entire area behind the house.

He looked to see the back door open. He stood for a moment at the screen door and heard voices inside. He smelled food. His mouth watered. But, the ache in the pit of his stomach went beyond just the need for food. His spirit was in need of nourishment.

Before the old man could knock, Colt raced up and flung open the squeaking screen door. "Howdy. Come in." Pop stepped inside, his first step tentative.

"Come on in and sit at the table," a woman's voice called out from down the hall and around the corner. "Colt'll show you the way. Dinner will be ready in just a minute."

Pop passed on through the tiny utility area and Marge Bradshaw appeared around the corner in the kitchen, transferring fried chicken from a skillet to a plate. He replied with a question. "Dinner, Ma'am?"

Marge continued pulling pieces from the hot oil, but smiled. "Oh, yes. You're in Texas now. We do dinner and supper, not lunch and dinner, Mister-" she paused then said, "I'm sorry. I don't know your last name."

Before he could answer, Colt blurted, "It's Peterson. But don't call him that. He doesn't like it."

Marge looked sternly at her son. "Colt, what have I told you about interrupting?"

"Sorry, Momma." He clasped his hands to his back and looked down at the floor.

"It's okay ma'am," Pop said, defending the youngster. "He's right. I do prefer being called Pop—"

"It's an *akraname*," Colt said, unable to hold back the new word he discovered, compelled to interject what he had learned.

Marge shook her head and smiled. "That boy. I swear," she said. "Go on, Colt. Get washed up for dinner."

Tom's waistline attested to Marge's cooking prowess and, as usual, dinner was excellent, yet she fretted over things not quite perfect. Pop hungrily devoured several helpings of chicken, mashed potatoes, gravy, biscuits and green beans. Quite literally, he ate until he could hold no more. When he finished, he squirmed nervously, trying not to make direct eye contact with anyone. He had not been concerned with etiquette for many years. Seldom had he been in situations where manners, of any kind, were called for.

Marge noticed his growing discomfort and attempted to make conversation. "I hope the food was to your liking."

"It was fine ma'am. But you might try a little sage and a couple pinches of cayenne pepper in the breading."

Tom abruptly stopped chewing and looked at his wife who returned a look of mild surprise.

"Thank you, Pop. I promise I'll give that a try real soon."

After Tom finished eating, he gave Pop a few simple instructions about how to go about his task in the field, adding that Colt would help by dragging the larger weeds out of the rows, once he had them cut.

Pop left the house and picked up a freshly sharpened hoe from the machine shed with Colt chattering at his side, as they walked toward the field. Pop's gait faltered, hampered by the stiffly starched pants. He reached around and pulled them from the crack of his butt.

"Curious fellow," Tom said, watching them walk away.

Marge joined her husband at the back door, thinking her own thought. "Remind me to get him a clean pair of underwear, too," she said.

FOUR

The afternoon passed quickly. Pop and Colt turned into an efficient weed elimination duo. The old man cut the weeds, the young man pulled them from the row of cotton stalks. Colt talked and asked questions. Pop might reply, or he might not. Colt was undeterred and persistent. Late in the afternoon Tom drove up on a tractor as they finished a couple of rows. "You fellas make a good team," he said. "But, let's save some for tomorrow. It'll be time to eat again soon."

The dinner routine repeated at supper, after which Pop went back to his quarters in the barn. The sun had set. Pop noticed how the cool of evening accentuated the musty smell of dust in the barn, an aroma that was surprisingly pleasant, unlike the stench of vacant warehouses in the Windy City that used to gnaw at him and provide its own brand of isolation. This didn't feel that way at all. Instead, he felt comfort in the aroma of the barn. It was a surprising twist because the odors were almost identical. He discovered his limbs didn't seem to ache as much, even after a hard afternoon in the field, figuring good nourishment fixed that problem.

On a bench near the door of his makeshift sleeping quarters, Pop saw a fresh towel and disposable razor. He added these items to his tiny stash of personal things he kept in a plastic grocery bag. Pulling his bottles of gin and pills from that sack, he set them on the floor near the old sofa. It was a habit. He always wanted them within arms reach. Unknowing of what the future held, it seemed reasonable, even now, to know there was a way out, if things became unbearable. But, on this night, it was little more than a formality.

He sauntered over and stood at the window, gazing into the night sky. Although the glass was hazed over with dust and cobwebs at the corners of every pane that undulated lazily with each breath, the sight that greeted him beyond was amazing and worth a lingering look. Though the nearest town was over ten miles away, he saw lights from neighboring towns all around. The terrain, featureless by day, provided spectacular views by night, unlike any he had ever seen. His eyes fixed on a slow blinking red beacon atop a tower far in the distance. Above that, more stars than he ever imagined could be seen in the night sky twinkled. All were sharply defined. As this mesmerizing view held his eyes, his mind recounted the events of the afternoon.

A five-year-old boy by the name of Rodney Oliver Bradshaw, whom he had come to know as Colt, possessed an innate sense of right, wrong, fairness and compassion. It's rare in adults, nearly nonexistent in a boy his age. He felt a subtle bonding process had begun. He wondered if it might simply be amusement with the lad.

While in the field, as it neared quitting time, Colt had told him a story about giving his daddy money for safekeeping. "You trusted him with your allowance, did ya?" he had joked with Colt.

"Oh, yes sir," the youngster said without hesitation, and quite seriously. "Daddy may not be all that pretty, but he is a good ol' boy, and I do trust him."

Pop stared into the night sky with his hands clasped behind him. He realized he was discovering an increasing number of things to smile about, all easily traced back to Colt. Slipping into a slower pace, his thoughts of the day changed to thoughts of sleep. He glanced back at the old sofa. It lured him. The night sky was worth every minute he spent at that window, but could do so no longer.

He fell upon the worn sofa willingly and stretched out. In a couple of short minutes, he drifted off. For the first time in years it was an easy transition that didn't include fond thoughts of sleeping pills or gin but of a young boy, almost six. His smile lingered. His sleep was laced with good dreams.

**

24

Over the next several days, Pop became indoctrinated into a strangely pleasant yet difficult existence called farm life. He and Colt had finished nearly a third of the field he was hired to clear of large, bothersome weeds. Color returned to his face. His features plumped with good health.

On this particular morning, the two worked their way to the end of a row and saw Tom wrestling with mechanical difficulty nearby. He had been shredding weeds in a ditch perpendicular to the cotton rows when the drive shaft on the shredder began to wallow and clank.

Pop saw him removing the bolts from a protective shroud to check out the problem, as he and Colt took a break for a drink of water. Taking a big swig from the insulated water jug, Colt wiped his face on his shirtsleeve. "What's the matter Daddy? Havin' trouble?" he asked, handing the jug to Pop. He marched as a boy on a mission to join his father.

"Yeah, I should've bought a new shredder in the spring, but I thought I could get one more year out of this one," Tom said, his drawl exaggerated, tugging at the formed sheet metal over the shaft.

Pop joined them, standing over Tom, just as the shroud was removed exposing the drive shaft. Reaching past Tom, he grabbed the shaft with one hand and shook it, making a quick diagnosis. "The needle bearings in the U-joint are shot." Without another word, he turned and walked back to the water jug for another drink.

Sitting back on his heels, Tom shoved his hat back with his thumb and said, "Pop, you've surprised me again. First you let me know you can cook and now it seems you're no dummy when it comes to things mechanical either."

Pop wiped his mouth with the back of his hand. "A man can't be on this earth as long as I've been and not pick up at least a few things."

"That's why I believe this man deserves a raise," Colt blurted. "Don't you, Daddy?"

Tom couldn't hide his embarrassment. "Well, now, Colt...I—"

"I only deserve what I've earned and no more," Pop said. He picked up his hoe and turned to Colt. "Come on, boy. I need to earn my keep, and you need to earn your allowance."

Keeping step curiously close to Pop, Colt resumed his incessant chatter. Response to it was only an occasional grunt. It didn't matter. Colt was comfortable with the old guy.

**

Ten days had passed since he'd arrived at the Bradshaw farm. At the pace he was going on the job he'd been given, it appeared that sometime during the eleventh day it would be finished.

Colt lost interest in his assigned task. He was more interested in chasing horned toads, throwing rocks, or doing just about *anything* that didn't include dragging weeds out of cotton rows. But, he provided a pleasant distraction. So, Pop removed the weeds as well as cut them with no complaint.

It was another typically hot August afternoon. The sky was filled with puffy cumulus clouds set against a crystal blue sky. Colt became fascinated with identifying faces and objects in the clouds. "That one looks like a horse. Look Pop. Don't you think so?" he cried. "Oh, and wow! That one over there looks like Mr. Bickley at the hardware store in Green Meadow. See the big nose? Golly, it looks just like him."

"Colt, did you know psychiatrists use blobs of ink on paper so that patients can tell them what they appear to be?" Pop slid down his hoe handle onto one knee to rest for a moment. "It helps the doctor understand what they're thinking and judge their mental condition better."

"What's a *sika trist*?" Colt asked, sitting beside him in the shade of a waist-high cotton stalk.

"A psychiatrist, Colt, is a doctor that helps people who can't think correctly," Pop explained. "Using the inkblot test is just one method for unlocking what's in the mind." He tapped his own temple with an index finger. "It gives the doctors

26

needed information to correct problems patients have developed."

Colt frowned, clearly puzzled and looking to Pop for answers.

"Look, I'll play a little game with you. It may help you understand," Pop said, going at it from a different angle. "I bet if I point at three clouds and you quickly tell me what they look like, I can tell you what you're going to be when you grow up." Pop dropped down into a fully seated position, crossing his extended legs. He leaned back, resting on his hands.

Clapping, Colt squealed, "Oh, boy. That sounds like fun." He settled down, mimicking Pop's sitting style and wiggled excitedly in anticipation.

Shielding his eyes from the sun, Pop searched the sky for the best examples. "Okay," he said, "What does that one look like?"

Colt's eyes followed the old man's pointing finger. "That looks like, umm, well, it looks sort of like a lot of people's heads," he said. "I can't see their bodies though. Maybe they're in a swimming pool. Which one next?"

Pop pointed to another, more elongated cloud. "All right. How about that one?"

"Oh, that's a road or maybe a railroad track. It's long, too. And, hey, it ends at the swimming pool where all the people are." Clearly believing he made a joke, he laughed.

"And one more..." Pop said slowly. He scanned the sky for an odd one. "How about that one over there? What does it look like?"

"Oh, that's an easy one. It's me on a big ol' crane lifting heavy stuff." He turned to the old man. His eyes grew large with anticipation, giving him full attention. "Okay, Pop. What am I going to be when I grow up?"

"Hang on a minute and let's examine what we have." Pop stroked his chin with the tips of his fingers. "The swimming pool could represent humanity in general, I suppose. The long road might indicate you'll be willing to travel far, or endure just about anything, to get to them. When you arrive

27

you'll use any means necessary to lift them out, even a big ol' crane."

"So, what am I going to be," Colt demanded impatiently, "a lifeguard, a truck driver or maybe run one of those neat rides at a carnival?"

With a grunt and a groan, Pop pulled himself up the hoe handle to his feet and said, "Nope. I think you're going to be a *sika trist*. And, judging by the improving condition of your first patient, I'd say you're going to be a darned good one."

"Huh?"

"Never mind." Pop dusted the seat of his pants, cut a weed then said, "Come on boy. We don't have much left. Let's get it done."

FIVE

The eleventh day dawned. Only a couple of hours work remained. A melancholy cloud followed Pop. He had grown accustomed to life at the Bradshaw farm. It didn't take long either. He became attached to the family, especially Colt, although he believed it a terrible mistake to allow the luxury of such extensive human contact. Memories of caring too much haunted him. Now, he steeled himself for the task ahead, which included the most difficult of all, leaving this place, and that boy, behind.

Getting out of bed earlier than usual, still nearly a half hour until the sun made its first appearance of the day; he walked to the machine shed and ground a new, sharper edge on his hoe. All the while, piecing together a game plan for when the job was done. He then headed for the field.

In the process of strengthening his resolve, he attacked the weeds with the appearance of exacting vengeance. It was inconsolable frustration that had to be put down and the weeds were the likely targets to get that done. Within two hours, he estimated, all that would be left was to ask for his money and a ride back to Green Meadow to wait for a southbound train.

Try as he might to exorcise his feelings, sadness dogged him. He slowed his pace, making it last longer than it should, stopping frequently to scan the ultra-clear skies, a signature sight of the Texas plains. Everything seemed to sparkle, distinctly defined at great distances.

An unusual sensation greeted his upturned face. It was the first tiny bite of autumn carried upon a September breeze. The wind suddenly swirled and, instead of pressing his front, it pushed at his back. It shifted and blew from a northerly direction. It brushed past his ears over his cheeks, as he methodically cut weeds then removed each one from the cotton rows. *Colt is probably still asleep,* he thought.

29

The sun was about to make its first appearance of the day to bathe the lingering dawn with its warmth. The eastern sky seemed to explode in hues of orange and pink, preparing to greet the sun.

Pop stopped momentarily to admire an optical illusion along the western horizon created by moisture in the air and just the right amount of light from the east. He distinctly saw the Sangre de Christo Mountains of eastern New Mexico upside down on the horizon, although the mountain range was over two hundred miles away. Other recognizable objects were clearly visible and inverted, seemingly suspended in midair, oil derricks, grain elevators, even a couple of small towns. It was one more intriguing thing Pop had grown accustomed to. He'd miss it.

He was so enthralled with the sight and so wrapped up in it, the first time he heard someone calling from a distance, he paid it no mind, figuring it was that breeze pushing past his ears, but when he heard it again, he recognized Colt's voice and spun around with a smile to greet his little companion. But Colt didn't appear happy.

The boy ran and tripped over every irregularity on the ground.

It quickly became obvious he was in a panic. "Pop!" he shouted, "You gotta come help! Somethin's wrong with Momma! She's on the floor. I can't wake her up!"

Pop dropped his hoe and ran toward Colt. "Where's your daddy, boy?"

"He took the shredder to get it fixed, but I don't know where." Colt sobbed. "You gotta hurry, Pop…you just gotta!"

Pop grabbed his hand. "Come on." They ran together back to the house.

Pop jumped the three steps onto the back porch and, in a single stride, had his hand on the screen door slinging it open as Colt cried, "She's in the kitchen."

Without breaking stride, Pop slid on the linoleum floor around the corner into the kitchen. The acrid smell of burning food filled the air. He hit a wall of dense smoke. He stopped to get his bearings. He snatched up a cup-towel from the near end of the kitchen counter and stepped into the smoke and lifted the skillet off a burner still blazing full tilt. He dropped it into the sink. He sprayed water on the super heated utensil, accidentally knocking a canister of flour to the floor, scattering it in a wide arc.

The skillet sizzled and spit over the surrounding countertop. Steam billowed.

He turned off the range and dropped down beside Marge below the smoky cloud. She lay on the floor on her side, knees drawn up. She clutched the fabric of her blouse over her chest. He pulled her hands away then rolled her gently onto her back and put his ear to her chest and listened for a heartbeat. It was extremely faint. Her breathing was rapid and shallow.

He sprang to his feet, turning to Colt. "Where are the keys to your Momma's car?"

"I don't know," Colt wailed, tears streaming from swollen eyes.

Pop grabbed the boy by the shoulders. "Think boy!"

Colt stopped crying abruptly and looked incredulously with wide eyes at Pop.

Pop tried again, this time more calmly. "Colt, where does your mother put her car keys after she comes through the back door?"

Colt wiped his tears away with one hand and pointed with the other at a plywood cutout of a large key hanging on the adjacent wall of the kitchen and utility area. In the center of a jumble of keys was a ring with a leather tab that had been embossed with the initials 'MB'.

He tossed the keys to Colt. "Here, you carry these. I'll carry your momma to the car."

Pop struggled. Marge was overweight and, given his age and slight build, it took everything he could muster to get her out of the house without harming her further.

Once he had her situated in the backseat of the car, he and Colt climbed in. Taking the keys from Colt, Pop gasped for one good breath of air, frantically studying the instrument panel. Fumbling the keys, he missed the ignition on his first attempt.

Salty sweat burned his eyes. With a shaky hand from overexertion and fear, he took a swipe across them to clear his vision. He then stabbed the correct one into the ignition lock and tried to turn it. It would not budge. Sweeping his hand over the steering column, he found the safety release and started the car. Grabbing the gear selector, he tried dropping it into reverse but it was locked as well. "What the hell?" he muttered.

Colt, still crying, "I think you have to put your foot on that pedal first." He pointed to the brake. "Daddy always said he didn't like all this new-fangled safety crap."

Pop would have smiled had it not been for the dire circumstances. Dropping it into gear, he over-accelerated in reverse. The car sprayed gravel. He steered hard in a one-eighty turn then slammed the selector into drive, repeating it going forward. They were enroute to the emergency room at the Bentley County Hospital in Green Meadow.

Tom noticed a rooster tail of brown dust coming from under a fast moving vehicle, far down the road, as he approached the driveway to his home. *Those folks are in a real big hurry. I wonder what that's all about?* He didn't dwell on it, hoping Marge still had breakfast ready, since he had left early. He was hungry. He was perturbed. Repair expense on the shredder was nearly double what he had anticipated. His mood deteriorated each time he remembered he had thought about replacing the shredder, but chose not to. *That was stupid—real damned stupid. Now it's going to cost about as much as a new one would have early in the spring before prices went up.* Pulling the old pickup truck up to his regular parking place, he noticed Marge's car gone. Furthermore, the skid marks on the graveled area behind the house where it usually set, indicated she must have left in a hurry.

Tom stood beside the pickup for a while, holding his Stetson and scratching his head. Then he noticed the back door stood wide open. Confusion was suddenly concern. He began to jog then broke into a run. Throwing the screen door open, he dashed into the kitchen.

The scene took his breath. Smoke lingered and the sickening smell of burned food assaulted his nose. Kneeling, he picked up Marge's glasses from the floor and stared in disbelief because she was never without her glasses. Flour slung across the flour indicated a possible struggle. "Oh, my God!" he shouted. "That sonofabitch kidnapped my wife and child!"

He called the sheriff's office, reported a kidnapping and hurriedly described the people and the car. The dispatcher encouraged him to remain calm and told him not to leave the house. "A deputy has been dispatched, Mr. Bradshaw. Please don't do anything before he gets there. Okay?" she told him. "An investigation will begin as soon as he arrives. Will you stay calm and remain at your house?"

Tom fidgeted and fussed. Then finally in a huff, "Okay, okay. I'll wait." It took tremendous willpower for Tom to sit and wait for someone to show up, since every instinct told him to load his deer rifle in the pickup and search for his family himself. Time wasted. Instead, he paced feverishly, growing angrier by the minute.

By the time a deputy arrived, Tom railed on Pop and how devious he must have been. Blaming, first, Pop, then himself for having trusted such a strange old man. The deputy didn't have much luck getting answers to his questions. Tom's analytical sense had drowned in raw emotion.

Suddenly, squelch broke on the deputy's car radio and a static-laced voice called, "Barry?" Before he could get to the handset the voice repeated, "Unit four, Barry?"

Keying the microphone, the officer responded. Tom kept an eye on him but paced to a fro with quick, choppy steps in front of the patrol car, mumbling contemptuously, kicking the ground.

"We've just had an emergency call from the Bentley County Hospital to locate Tom Bradshaw," the dispatcher said. "Isn't that where you are right now?"

Tom stopped abruptly when he heard his name and watched the deputy but could not understand the conversation he heard. Nostrils flared, he continued to fume.

"Mr. Bradshaw," the deputy told him, "We've received an urgent call to locate you because your wife has been taken to the hospital for emergency medical attention."

Tom's anger stayed at fever pitch but amended with trepidation and concern. "Where is she? "What's wrong with her?"

"Mr. Bradshaw—"

"God Damn it! What's wrong with her, I said?"

"Please, calm down and get in my car. I'll take you there. I don't think you should be driving in your agitated state."

Within seconds, they were speeding into town, lights flashing, siren wailing. Still, Tom thought it took too long to get to the hospital. He had the car door open before the deputy screeched to a stop at the emergency room door. He leaped out. He ran, sliding sideways through the automatically opening double doors because they parted too slow to suit him. By the time he negotiated his way through various orderlies, nurses and doctors, he saw Marge, down the hall, lying on a gurney with an intravenous drip in her arm and a tube up her nose. She was wheeled into intensive care with alarming speed. He ran to catch up, but was stopped by a hand that snared his arm.

It was the ER doctor. "Mr. Bradshaw?"

Breathing heavily, Tom's eyes remained fixed on Marge disappearing into a room. "Yeah. I'm Tom Bradshaw," he said, huffing.

"Your wife has had a severe heart attack," the doctor told him. And if it hadn't been for this gentleman it may have been even worse." He pointed to Pop sitting quietly in one of the chairs lining the hallway.

The old man's shirt was sweat-soaked. He was visibly exhausted. He sat with his legs extended and parted, his arms hanging loosely, staring without expression toward the door Marge had just been wheeled through. As yet, he had not caught his breath either.

"Mr. Bradshaw, are you going to be okay?" the doctor asked. "You look as though you might need to sit down."

Tom stared at the old man; mouth agape, as all suspicions came crashing in on him. When Pop's eyes met his, he attempted to thank him. His voice failed. Only a squeak escaped his throat. As he tried to force it, he choked on his own words. The only one he managed was, "Colt?"

"A nurse is sitting with him in the cafeteria," Pop told him.

Tom turned away in shame, unable to look the old man in the eye.

SIX

Why can't I move on, get past it, put it out of my mind? It was natural to believe what I saw. Right? All the evidence supported it. It looked like there'd been a struggled. Didn't it? Besides, my mood wasn't the greatest even before I discovered the aftermath in the kitchen. Anyone would have believed the same. Wouldn't they? Tom tried many times, many ways, to rationalize his reaction. It simply did not work. His sense of personal responsibility simmered and occasionally bubbled into all-out self-recrimination. Those episodes were on the increase. The weight of his own questions crushed him. He became consumed with guilt. His adversary was hindsight and that was like swatting at a bat in the dark.

He waged a battle against an unbeatable foe. Although he lost ground against it, he would not be flying any white flag. The internal debate raged. He wanted to blame someone, or something, when, in fact, there was neither. In the end, when it finally occurred to Tom that it simply could not be beaten, he turned on the easiest target of all—himself. The blame game slipped into overdrive.

Of course, Tom Bradshaw was a natural worrier. He was a farmer. He tortured himself, remembering the harshness of what he had thought and said, knowing he should do something to make it right with the old guy. His peace of mind was at stake. No amount of rationalizing erased that guilt. The fact Pop had no knowledge of what Tom had suspected did not play into it. Tom was as virtuous as a Texas farmer could get, determined to do the right thing. He was not the sort to see the situation any other way.

Sitting on the edge of the hospital bed, he stroked Marge's hand as she slept. She drew deep, even breaths. She had regained consciousness late the previous evening, but kept sedated so she could sleep. Her condition remained serious but she was stable. Healing would be long and slow but the

37

prognosis was good for a full recovery that promised a long life. She would be eating differently and taking regular medications but life, eventually, should return to normal at the Bradshaw home.

He wished he could talk to her about it. She'd have the perfect answer; he just knew it. She always did. But, Tom also knew he could not burden her with his guilt even if she were awake. It was a problem he would have to figure out for himself.

"Mr. Bradshaw..."

Startled, he turned to see an elderly nurse peeking around a partially opened door. He smiled, but it lacked sincerity. "I'm sorry. My mind was elsewhere."

"I could tell," she said, displaying the Texas Plains trademark of water-stained teeth in her own broad smile. "Your son Colt wanted me to ask if it was okay if he and that fella he calls Pop could take the car home." She snickered. "He wanted the old guy to prove he could cook, and fix his dinner. That young'un talks so adult for a little guy."

A courteous half-smile lifted a corner of Tom's mouth. "Yeah. He does." He suddenly remembered Pop's suggestion to Marge on how she might improve her fried chicken.

As Pop had prepared to leave Marge's hospital room the morning before, he volunteered to watch Colt. Tom handed him some cash and he rented a room across the street in a small motel so they could stay within easy walking distance and, possibly, provide a place Tom could rest, though he never did. "Yeah", Tom said then repeated with more enthusiasm, "Yeah, I think that would be a great idea and, if you don't mind relaying the message, tell Pop to move all his stuff into the spare bedroom inside the house."

She looked quizzically at him for a moment. "Whatever you say, Mr. Bradshaw," she said and began to withdraw from the room, stopping suddenly and stepping back in. "One more thing; I know you came in with Deputy Brown yesterday, so I can have one of the orderlies drive you home later in one of the hospital vans, if you like."

Nodding, "Thanks. That'd be great." He turned back to Marge.

"I'll arrange it right now," the nurse said.

Still stroking her hand, Tom thought how a simple request by Colt had spawned a possible solution, a healing salve for his guilt. "Ya know Marge," he whispered, "sometimes I think Colt is a very wise old man trapped inside a five year old body."

**

By the time the orderly dropped Tom off at home it was dark. Tom was painfully aware of his near-debilitating fatigue. He opened the door of the hospital van and stepped out, but his exit could more aptly be described as falling out.

Thanking the young man for the ride, he slammed the door, tapped it with a palm and waved a friendly goodbye. As the van rolled down the driveway, he turned to look toward the light from the open back door of the house, and took a moment to understand the symbolism in that, otherwise, mundane view of the back of his home. Fireflies danced in the periphery of the yellow glow through the screen door. Frogs down by the stock tank sang their evening song and crickets provided backup. The air hinted crisp cleanliness. The whole picture, sound and all, was a welcoming beacon that nearly lifted him from his feet. He suddenly felt blessed.

He heard banter between a matter-of-fact old guy and an overly inquisitive five-year-old, about to turn six.

Not quite ready to engage anything other than his improving mood, he turned back to the night sky overlooking the farm that gently fell away from the backyard. The moon was a brilliant blue-gray in a very clear sky. There were so many stars it was amazing the sky could hold them all. It was the perfect early autumn night, as the dry air of the Texas plains chilled quickly after sunset. Tom shivered slightly, when a light breeze caressed his bare neck.

The lonesome call of a single coyote, far in the distance, was a prompt. It was time to go inside and rest. Tom trudged slowly on swollen, stiff legs, feeling the ache of exhaustion with each step. The porch was a mere three steps up, but a formidable obstacle on this night. Taking a deep breath with each step, he reached for the screen door, feeling the warmth radiating from the house to greet him.

When he let the rickety old screen door slam behind him, the talk from the kitchen stopped abruptly and Colt came running around the corner, down the hall, straight into his daddy's arms. Tom squeezed the tyke hard, lifting him high and growled. As he swung the boy around, his short legs flagged out. "Have you been a good boy?"

"Sure." Colt dismissed the question. "Momma? How's Momma? Is she gonna be awright?"

Lowering the boy to the floor, he straightened his shirt, now bunched around his shoulders. Tom sat down on his heels and looked Colt directly in the eyes. "The Doctor said your momma is going to be just fine," he said, "but she needs a lot of rest when she gets home. So, you and me, little man, have to make it easy for her to heal. Do you think you can help her around the house and do all your chores without being asked?"

Colt drew a broad, knowing grin and grabbed his daddy's hand. "Come on. Let's eat and we can talk about that."

Tom tossed his hat onto a hook in the back hall with an adroit flip of his wrist. In the dining room, Pop sat patiently at the aging chrome and Formica topped table, waiting for them to come in and sit down. Tom stopped and stared in amazement at the spread on the table. A large platter was heaped with pork chops that had been corn breaded and fried. A bowl full of steaming broccoli had a cheese sauce oozing over its top. Still another bowl was filled with a salad chock full of quartered tomatoes. "There were a few tomatoes left on those vines in the garden," Pop said, when he noticed Tom staring at it. "It seems a frost may be coming soon, so I didn't see the point in letting them go to waste."

Tom helped Colt into his chair. "Nothing tastes better than the first tomatoes in the spring, and the last few in the fall," he said, taking his regular seat at the head of the table.

Tom had not realized just how hungry he was, until he began to eat. What he did realize from the start was that Pop did, in fact, know how to cook. *Why would a man who can cook like this, plus, have mechanical know-how and—God knows what else—choose to be a homeless drifter?* He could not figure it out. But it was a question that would remain in his thoughts because he realized it just was not any of his business to know and rude if he asked. With every delicious bite, his curiosity heightened. He was intrigued by the old guy and wanted to know more about him, but the unspoken Texas code of conduct prevented him from asking those questions. The one holding the secrets was the only person that had the right to share them, and should never be asked to do so. And, that's just the way it was.

Tom looked across at Pop. He hunkered over his plate with both elbows on the table, holding a pork chop with both hands. He devoured it, both cheeks crammed to capacity with meat, eating as though it might be his last food for a while. There were cornmeal crumbs and grease at the corners of his mouth and bits of breading and broccoli scattered on the table beside the plate. Tom snapped a grin but let it go before he could be noticed. *He might know how to cook, but table manners have passed him by.*

Colt rearranged food on his plate. It appeared he had thoughts of his own. "Daddy, Pop said he was leaving tomorrow. I told him I wanted him to stay but he told me it was *nessry.*"

"Necessary. The word is pronounced *nes-ah-sary,*" Pop corrected, without looking up from his plate.

"That's what I said, *nessry,*" he responded, then turned back to his daddy, "I don't want him to go."

Tom sat straight and quietly chewed the inside of his cheek for a moment. Then focused on Pop. "Why must it be necessary?" he asked the old man.

"I've heard winters are usually very cold in this part of Texas. I've even heard you mention it, Mr. Bradshaw," Pop said with a full mouth, spitting a few crumbs, "I can't be

41

trapped this far north with no money and no place to stay. I need to find a warmer climate, maybe Houston."

He washed his food down with a big gulp of iced tea.

"Is that what *nessry* means, Daddy?"

Tom reached over and placed a hand on Colt's hand to quiet him. "I've been thinking. Obviously our situation has dramatically changed," he said, gesturing toward Marge's empty chair. "I have harvest coming up in about a month and Marge will be recuperating and doesn't need to be worrying about things, and Colt registers to start school next week." His hand went from Colt's hand to the top of the boy's head and jostled his hair. "Colt may think I'm Superman, but I certainly know better. When that cotton out there is ready, it'll demand all my attention until its gathered and sitting in the gin yard. Time is of the essence in farming and if time is lost in the field our livelihood may go with it."

He paused, took a sip of ice tea then pursed his lips into a serious frame. "Pop, I don't have the luxury to hesitate or be ashamed. I need help. Would you consider staying on through the winter with us?"

Pop became visibly uncomfortable, swallowing hard. For the first time since Tom arrived home from the hospital, the old man made eye contact. "Well I'm not...what I mean is—"

"Before you give me an answer," Tom said, holding his hand up, "I want you to know the spare bedroom would be yours and I would personally guarantee you a weekly paycheck until at least spring planting time, which would be late April or early May." He paused and shrugged. "Of course I can't say exactly what your job description would be, but it would center around taking care of the house, cooking and looking after Colt."

An uncomfortable silence fell over the table. Colt appeared to be holding his breath. Tom stared at Pop, waiting for an answer.

As for Pop, he sucked air between his teeth and looked away from Tom but held a thoughtful gaze on Colt.

"What's the matter Pop? Don't you think I'm worth it?" Colt asked, grinning.

With only a hint of smile, "You might be, boy. You just might be."

SEVEN

Pop successfully evaded the question of staying. He did not offer any commitments. But his actions implied that he would. He moved his meager worldly possessions into the Bradshaw's home. From the moment he entered the back door, taking up residence in the spare bedroom as the goal, he had a strange flutter in his stomach, almost queasy. It was strongly symbolic of permanence. It scared him. Moving in with the family marked the beginning of redefining who he was, maybe his attitude and outlook, too, but his rituals, hardened by years of habit, would take time.

Moving things into that bedroom was only the beginning. Things became knee-jerk, one hesitation was followed by another. The first evening, he cleaned the supper dishes and went to his new quarters, the guest room just off the kitchen. He stood at the door and thought on what it meant once he crossed that threshold. It was disquieting, although he took comfort knowing Colt's room was between his own and the youngster's parents' room.

Unaccustomed to such a meticulous arrangement, the pristinely neat surroundings kept Pop off balance, even a bit clumsy, fearing he might upset the order of things. A woman's touch was everywhere in the room. Doilies were atop every flat surface and, on a small three-legged table, tucked in a corner, there set a small wooden bowl of potpourri sweetening the air. The bed was made precisely. Wrinkles would not dare appear. The worn wooden furniture gave silent testimony to many years of use, but his reflection affirmed the love and care in each glossy surface. The gingham curtains, adorning the only window, flaunted ruffles, tied back precisely with a matching strip of cloth.

He even began doing things—little things that he hadn't given thought to in years, like checking his feet for mud or grease when he entered the house, checking his hands before he

45

touched anything; even checking himself in the mirror before sitting down to a meal. It was the reinvention of self that kept him off balance.

Now, as he stood in his room, his eyes were drawn to the translucent skin of the tattered plastic grocery bag on the bed. The contents were not clearly visible, but he intimately knew every item inside. For several long seconds, it remained untouched. He struggled with a decision. Believing that if he took those few possessions from the sack, it was a commitment, *but* if he left them in the bag, he still had the option to leave.

Though the action was largely a mind game, for Pop the decision to unpack his meager possessions carried great weight and responsibility. After all, he had not agreed definitively to Tom's proposition; he had only implied that he would stay. Pop was not comfortable making promises that could bind him beyond a few days. His ingrained sense of right and wrong would not allow him to go back on anything he might promise. A promise to the old guy was more than a simple verbalization of *okay*. It was a sacred vow, a serious matter indeed. He had not made a promise to anyone for anything in about a quarter century. For as long, he had actively avoided situations that called for him to be responsible for anybody. The pain of failing such a commitment was more than he ever intended to take on again. He grappled with the notion of becoming part of a family he had only known for a couple of weeks then staying for six to nine months. The worry lines deepened, as he contemplated the pros and cons, his eyes remained fixed on that tattered grocery bag, laid in the center of a neatly made bed— the bed covered over with a spread adorned with the print of orchids and oleanders, not a man's room at all. At this crossroads, that little bag symbolized everything he was, or had been, for over two decades.

"Tom seems to be a pretty straight-up guy," he mumbled, absent-mindedly pushing the long thin hair from his forehead. "And, it's true that he can't handle both the farming operation and the household without help." Pop's eyes locked onto the bag on the bed. He conjured an image of Marge lying helpless in the hospital. *She's a good woman. Not only would she be of no help to the family or farm, she'd need considerable attention herself over the coming weeks and months, most likely.* Still he was unconvinced. The worry lines deep and unchanged.

An internal battle waged that could result in a metamorphosis, a change in his life that involved a giant leap of faith. That fiercely independent part of him argued in favor of not becoming attached to anyone, or anything, as a necessary way to live—more importantly, he believed, vital to survival. He vowed long ago to never again take on or develop encumbrances. Commitments opened him up to pain and emotional conflict of a sort he was not sure he ever wanted to chance coping with again.

Serious, life-altering questions needed answers. *Am I willing to go back on that promise? Do I want to change the course of my life? How hard will it be when it finally comes time to leave? Do I really want to tackle this at this late stage of my life? No. I don't think I can handle it. I think I should sever this bond and move on...soon. It's necessary.*

"Necessary," he whispered, contemplating the weight of a single word. The lines of his face relaxed. He thought of Colt.

"Is it really necessary? Maybe leaving isn't all that *nessry.*" He smiled, then he thought back to a moment he had had sitting on a bench on the courthouse square wondering if he might find happiness in such a remote place as Green Meadow, Texas.

Pop reached for the bag, hesitantly at first, and then with gusto he dumped the contents onto the bed. He put the few scraps of clothing, his newly acquired disposable razor and other items in the top drawer of a nearby four-drawer chest. Then placed the small bottle of gin and the bottle of pills back inside the bag, wrapping it tightly and putting it out of sight, in a small drawer beside the bed. The type of comfort those items offered had no lure this night.

His future remained uncertain and, as yet, did not have the courage to be without those things. He felt compelled to keep them close at hand, but out of sight. He felt some embarrassment and a touch of revulsion that he kept them at all, but he did.

**

The days that followed were a blur of activity on the Bradshaw farm.

Tom had more things to do than he had time for. He focused on getting the cumbersome mechanical cotton picker ready for harvest, belts and bearings replaced, and cracks welded. The fall season was a tense time on the Texas plains. Farmers raced the weather and rapidly changing market conditions, doing everything possible to gain an edge that promised a good crop at a good price. The first cotton of the season could be sold at the best price before the market could be flooded with the incoming commodity. Everyone wanted that early harvest.

Tom attacked every task with a hint of desperation, knowing that the window of opportunity for a successful harvest was fleeting. Also fleeting were moments of joy. There could be no laughter or merry-making until all the hard work of the entire year was brought to a successful conclusion. He hurriedly lubricated every moving part and did everything he could think of to ensure trouble-free operation of the aging mechanical cotton-picker. It was no less important than an airline mechanic on a pre-flight check. Lives were dependent on things functioning as they should. He only had the one cotton-picker and it had to run flawlessly throughout the entire harvesting process. Once begun, he could not stop until all the cotton was safely in the hands of the ginner.

The farm also boasted nearly seventy-five acres of sorghum grain, but Tom had hired a traveling crew with their own equipment to harvest that, although it demanded some of his time to oversee that it was done properly. He constantly monitored the process to be sure the combines kept running and dump trucks were continuously hauling newly cut grain to the elevator in Green Meadow. He had worked hard during the growing season. It was not the time to leave anything to chance. Rest could only come during the cold, snowy days of winter, after all cotton and grain were harvested, sold, or, at the very least, in storage and ready to sell.

The first blue-northern of the season swept across the plains and dropped temperatures into the twenties. It was bitterly cold and windy for a single day and, although the air was raw and biting, it was not an unwelcome event to a farmer, rather it was an expected rite of passage serving as a positive demarcation between the growing season and the harvest season.

Furthermore, the collective mood of the community lightened, for a time, with the first hard freeze of the year, since freezing temperatures defoliated cotton stalks and dried the plants, so bolls popped open quickly, exposing the pure white of new cotton. A hard freeze also made the stalks brittle so harvesting would be easier and the dry cotton could be sucked from the open bolls easily. Green leaves and stalks were a nuisance that clogged machinery. Cold temperatures also aided the grain crop to lose some of its moisture content. Prices would be docked if the moisture content were too high. For a while after a timely hard freeze, farmers laughed and joked but, then, they were all business all over again. A blast of frigid air tumbling southward was a positive event. Things came together nicely, but time was of the essence and the focus had to be on getting crops out of the field before the fickle Texas weather dictated any other course of action. Temperatures warmed rapidly and a period of Indian summer seemed imminent, but a fast-approaching secondary front chilled it right back down. So went the seasons' battle for dominance.

Pop quickly learned the intricacies of managing a household, especially within the confines of a strange schedule dictated by farming events. He was trusted with the family car to drive into Green Meadow to buy groceries and help Colt pick out school clothes. He came to be recognized as the Bradshaw's hired hand around town. Respect for the old guy rose, as word spread through the community that he was solely responsible for saving Marge Bradshaw's life.

Since he limited driving to and from Green Meadow, local law enforcement conveniently overlooked the fact he did not carry a driver's license. Seeing their leniency as a quiet collective thank you for his unselfish act. People who, at first, passed him by and refused eye contact, now smiled and spoke. Some even called him Pop in a friendly homespun way.

Eight days had passed since Marge was admitted to the hospital. She lost over twenty pounds and the pallor of her skin was another testament of her condition. She was too weak to walk, but the doctors had done all they could and a lengthy period of recuperation was the only factor remaining in her full recovery. It was time for her to go home.

Tom took a day off to spend precious time with her on the day of her return. He was nervous as he showered and dressed. It was the same feeling he had had the day of his first date with Marge so many years ago. He thought fondly of that, as he made ready to leave the house. Each time he stroked his face with a razor, a new spot of blood appeared. He could not help being careless. His mind refused to be in the moment. He was about to go after his favorite girl, his sweetheart, and bring her home. Unfortunately, he had great difficulty focusing. His attention was fractured, skipping from this to that, like frogs jumping from one lily pad to the next. The farm would just have to wait but he could not stop the worry.

Pop was busy in the kitchen cleaning up the breakfast mess and Colt played on the floor with a toy combine and a small dump truck, pretending to help with the harvest. The smell of pancakes lingered in the air and the constant whir of the heating system seemed extra pleasant, set against the strong northerly wind howling outside.

Each time something undone crossed Tom's mind, he yelled it from the bathroom as a question, or comment up for grabs. "We need to move that ol' mother cow off the pasture into a pen today. She'll be calving soon. It'll be too cold if she drops it in the pasture. A newborn probably wouldn't survive."

The shock of stinging aftershave slapped on his face precipitated another thought. "We also need to see if the combine crew needs help driving grain trucks to the elevator. I

50

think they've lost one, maybe two, of their hired help." Before that statement cleared his lips, he was thunderstruck with another potential problem. "Dadgummit! I almost forgot. We still need to drop by the John Deere House in Green Meadow and get those new bearings for that damned cotton picker." He fell forward resting his hands on the bathroom sink, overwhelmed. Movement beyond the open door caught his attention. He looked up. It was Pop.

"Mr. Bradshaw," he said, smacking his lips, "here's what I'll do today and you be sure and tell me if it's not satisfactory."

Tom stood straight and squared his body with Pop, examining the old man, whose physical appearance had changed remarkably since moving into the house. Pop's hair was combed. Tom studied his clean-shaven face for a moment. "Okay. Shoot."

"I'll leave in a few minutes and drop Colt off at school. By that time the John Deere House should be open. I'll pick up those bearings, if you'll write the part number on a piece of paper. Once I get back here, I'll herd that mother cow into the pen and make sure she has feed. Then I'll drive down to the grain field. By that time they should have one, or more, loaded trucks ready to be emptied. I'll drive them into Green Meadow and dump them at the elevator. In the meantime, Mr. Bradshaw, you concentrate on getting your wife home safely."

And, with that, Pop turned and walked back toward the kitchen without waiting for a response.

Tom exhaled loudly. Pent up dread drained away. *Damn! The value of that man's stock just shot way up.*

**

"You know what, Pop?" Colt broke the silence.

"What, boy?" Pop asked as he concentrated on the heavily rutted section line dirt road. Sand streamed over the road and drifted across into the ditch, wind pushed against the side of the car. He clutched the steering wheel with both hands, stretching a little to see over it.

51

"I think you oughta just move in with us *forever*," Colt said, his conviction firm.

Pop turned the family sedan onto the street that ended at the elementary school. He glanced over for a split second then looked to the road ahead. "Can't do that," he said. "It would be an unwelcome intrusion into family tradition."

"*Trishun*. What's *trishun*?"

A crooked smile pulled up on the left side of Pop's mouth. "Not *trishun* boy. The word is *tra-dishun*." He glanced over again. "Tradition is something people do on a regular basis and it becomes customary." He stopped near the front door of the school.

"I don't understand, Pop."

The old man reached across Colt's lap and opened the passenger side door, shoving it open. "You get out and go on to school now. We'll talk more about it later. Okay?"

"You betcha." He leaped out, waving at friends, and off he ran.

Pop took a moment to savor the sight of Colt, in his world.

**

It was a long, slow ordeal getting Marge from the hospital home since she was so weak. There was little she could do to help with her own mobility. Bedridden so long, her muscles had atrophied.

Tom had the help of two burly orderlies while still at the hospital, helping transfer her from the wheel chair into the cab of the pickup truck. But he had no help when they arrived home. Her extremely weakened condition caused him anxious moments, as he attempted to move her into the house without injuring her further. It was past midday when he finally had her comfortably in bed. As for Marge, she was overly emotional, thankful just to be alive. Resting at home and not in a hospital was a small blessing, but it was enough. It washed over her and she wept softly. She shared that there were a few times in the hospital she questioned if she would ever be with her family again. She ran her fingers over the lace-edge pillowcases, smoothing her favorite bedspread over her body.

Tom opened the drapes so she could see out. Daylight filled every corner of the room and added cheeriness. Outside, high wispy clouds covered the sky. The wind blew in gusts, whipping streamers of sand passed her window.

That didn't matter. It was a beautiful sight to her. She breathed in the sight and feel of the moment.

Tom sat in a chair beside the bed and, after they shared lunch on a single tray, they carried on light conversation for a long while. Tom avoided stressful topics, choosing instead to talk about Colt, school and the good job Pop was doing. Time slipped into late afternoon. He noticed Marge looking past him through the window. Following her gaze he noticed a loaded grain truck moving slowly down the turnrow on the backside of the farm. Daylight ebbed, shadows lengthened. Days became shorter. The sight of the grain truck sucked him back into the harsh reality of harvest and how the most precious commodity of all—time—slipped by.

The change in his expression did not go unnoticed. "You go on and do what you need to do, Tom," she said. "I'll be fine."

He did not respond immediately, just nodded. "Okay. I'll relieve Pop and send him back here to start supper."

Even after having said it, he was hesitant to leave for even that short time, but when the squealing brakes of the school bus caught his attention he relaxed. Colt could visit with her until Pop made it back to the house.

∗∗

The day ended on a successful note. The combine crew finished cutting the grain. It had all been delivered to the safekeeping of the grain elevator in Green Meadow. Tom opted to sell a portion of it immediately at the current market price. The first income of the year relaxed him, but just a little.

A new calf had been born in the relative warmth of a protective shed, making the weather a non-issue in its prospects for survival. The cold front that brought clouds and wind pushed south, leaving behind a beautiful night of calm, stars, and a full moon—a harvest moon.

Pop settled in during the early evening hours and found a medical encyclopedia on a nearby shelf. He passed the time in a corner of the living room studying it. He claimed squatter's rights on an out-of-the-way chair used little by the family. The lack of wind outside created an unusual but welcomed quiet inside the house. It was a much-needed atmosphere for rest.

Colt played on the floor with plastic cowboys and Indians and Tom broke an extended silence when he looked over his newspaper and said, "Colt, go tell your momma good night and come right back here."

"Can I climb into bed with her so she can tell me a story?"

Tom raised the paper, preparing to continue reading. "No, just tell her good night and come back."

"Aw, Daddy. Please."

Agitated, Tom noisily dropped the paper into his lap. "Colt! Don't argue! Just do what I told you!"

Suddenness and anger combined to shock Colt. He couldn't understand why his daddy would shout at him. Lip quivering, he stared in disbelief at his father. His face screwed into a pained look and tears trickled down his cheeks.

Pop placed his book on a nearby table. He knew that the boy could not grasp the severity of his mother's illness, and it didn't help matters that Tom was too tired to explain why he was on edge. "Come on Colt," he said, "Let's go start a tradition before you have to go to bed."

Colt sat on the floor rubbing the tears from his eyes, clearly fighting the urge to cry. He pushed his lower lip out, whimpering. Reaching up, he took the old man's hand.

Pop opened the front door of the house and both walked out onto the porch into the cold night. Every breath turned white, as warm air met cold. Pop lifted Colt and sat him atop the short porch railing facing the brilliant silvery moon. "I promised you this morning that I'd try to better explain what a tradition is," he said. "The best way to do that is to start one."

Standing behind Colt, he placed a hand on each shoulder. "This will be our tradition. But you have to promise to keep it up, or it won't be a tradition. Can you promise that?"

Still rubbing his eyes, Colt sniffed and looked up at Pop. He nodded. His lower lip quivered.

Pop struck a thoughtful pose and sighed, trying to come up with the right words. Suddenly, from out of his past, a children's story he once heard came to mind. Finally, "No matter how far we may drift apart, we can always be together, here." He placed a finger over his heart. "And here." He touched his head. "We can always be together this way. We can make *our* tradition special moments to share fond memories."

He pointed to the full moon that seemed to cover an inordinate amount of the autumn sky and every feature of its surface clearly defined. "By looking skyward any clear night and saying *Pleasant dreams and sleep tight—Good night Mr. Moon—Good night.* We can be together, instantly…to share what's on our minds." He looked down at Colt. "This will be our own special key to unlock the link that's ours…just you and me, no one else. You can talk to me, and I can talk to you— anytime, anywhere. This will be our tradition. Okay?"

Colt looked away from Pop to the brilliance of the moon's surface, wiped away a tear and whispered, "Pleasant dreams and sleep tight…" He paused and looked up at Pop.

"That's right. Go on."

Colt stammered, "G-Good night Mr. Moon. Goodnight." He sniffed one more time then tilted his head until his cheek touched Pop's hand that rested upon his shoulder.

EIGHT

Harvest was over. Crops were out of the fields and the land across the north Texas plains lay bare and at rest. The blustery days of autumn passed into colder but calmer days of winter at the Bradshaw farm.

The entire Green Meadow community took on a gentler personality, as Christmas approached.

A comfortable pattern evolved allowing Tom Bradshaw time to take care of farm business and not worry about Colt. Pop did a commendable job, gaining full trust of the Bradshaw family.

Marge became stronger, day-by-day, step-by-step, capable of doing more than Tom allowed. She carefully guarded against resentment of his overly restrictive attitude. She felt cabin fever had become more the problem than over-exertion. The stress of doing nothing, itself, tightened her chest. She had to get out, be active, up and around, a vital member of the family and the community, not an invalid. His stubbornness tested her patience. It bordered on anger.

He doted, still harboring guilt for not being around when she fell ill. Whenever he found her doing anything that appeared strenuous he put a halt to it and a shiver usually followed, when he considered what might have happened if Pop had not been around that fateful day.

On a cold Saturday morning in mid-December, as Tom was about to leave the house to feed livestock, Marge announced she was going to town to Christmas shop. She wanted no argument on the matter. The sudden statement took Tom by surprise. He argued anyway. Reluctantly, he gave in to her wish, as long as he could go with her.

Marge stiffened her back. "No." It was firm and the answer stood alone and strong between them. "I don't want you to go."

"You don't want me around?"   He was hurt and confused.

"It's not that, Tom," she said, now smiling. "I just need time away from the house, and you have things to do." She gave his arm a patronizing pat. "I love you so much my healing heart is full, but, Tom Bradshaw, if you don't loosen your grip on me that same heart is going to explode in my chest." She held his chin and forced unblinking eye contact until he gave her an answer she would accept.

He started to speak, but then just looked at her, confused.

"Oh, for Pete's sake, Tom, wipe that puppy dog look off your face. I'll be fine, and so will you, just go about your business. Please."

Tom placed a single finger under the brim of his felt Stetson and shoved it away from his face until it was barely hanging from the back of his head. "Okay," he said, "but I insist that Pop drive you, and Colt go along, too, to help carry things."

She shrugged and flashed a wide smile. "I can live with that."

The ride into Green Meadow was pleasant but conversation was subdued. Pop concentrated on the road ahead while Colt stared out the window at the passing countryside.

Marge planned her day. Suddenly, and with a sly smile, she reached into her purse and took out a fifty-dollar bill. She shoved it into Pop's shirt pocket.

Pop snapped a glance at her fingers in his pocket then at her. "I don't understand, Ma'am."

"I know what Tom told you to do today, but I'm going to ask you to handle it differently." She paused, watching Pop's face for signs of protest with all the patience of a first grade school teacher.

"Go on," he said, looking back down the road. "What's the plan?"

"I want you to take Colt and y'all have lunch at the diner. Then go to an afternoon matinee at the theatre. Simply put, I need to be away from the house for a while and you two need time away from me."

Without argument, Pop simply stopped in downtown Green Meadow, on the square and said, "We'll be back, right here at this spot, in three hours," he said. "Is that enough time?"

Marge nodded briskly. "Thanks Pop." She gave him a friendly squeeze on the elbow then turned and placed a finger on Colt's nose. "Our secret?"

Colt giggled and nodded enthusiastically. He was excited. He beamed with pride. Secrets were wonderful fun, a game he relished having been chosen to be part of. He puffed out his chest. "You betcha. Our secret. You, me and Pop."

As the two walked the square looking into brightly decorated storefront windows, they talked over possibilities of what might be under the tree Christmas morning. Colt talked nonstop, asking questions about everything that crossed his mind. The breeze was light but cold. White clouds of frosty air huffed from every mouth and nose out on the sidewalk. Pop listened with feigned interest in what the boy said but there was nothing fake about his interest in Colt. That was genuine. He gladly lent his ear to anything the youngster had to say. He was patient, responding just enough to pacify the boy. When they walked down the sidewalk together, Colt stayed so close to Pop's leg that the old man had occasional trouble with his gait. The little guy hung tight to his best friend, looking straight up at Pop, chattering all the while.

The diner seemed to be a popular place at lunchtime on that cold December Saturday. It was the same diner that refused him service when he first arrived in Green Meadow—in fact, the only diner. But, even as he stepped through the door, he felt the difference. An inviting rush of comforting warmth greeted him, along with noticeable changes in attitudes towards his presence. The gap-toothed old lady behind the counter smiled, instantly friendly and talkative. Her gray hair was in a bun but errant strands dangled down both cheeks. Her husband, the overweight ex-Marine, evidenced by the USMC tattoo on his forearm, even had kind words and a joke for him. The place buzzed with conversations. Dishes and silverware rattled and clanked, nearly creating a harmony. It reminded Pop of a song he could not quite identify. There was definitely a holiday feel and friendliness in the air. Pop felt a twinge of envy and even a tiny ache in his heart that someday, not that far in the future, he'd have to leave.

The signs of a close-knit community were everywhere. People talked from table to table, even calling out across the room on occasion. "Hey, Harv. Bobby Joe told me that first bale premium you got at the gin was substantial," one shouted across to another table. From the other end of the diner, "Hey, Emma, Leroy hinted that *Santy* Claus might be extra good to you this year," another yelled out with a wink and a laugh."

Pop knew he was tolerated and accepted, but only as a visitor. He longed for that sense of belonging he saw and felt all around him—a type that was not that much different than within the Bradshaw family, just extended to include the whole town. In essence, he was still on the outside looking in, just like all those storefront windows he and Colt ogled. It was a look-but-do-not-touch sensation. The only difference now, over when he arrived, was that he looked a little better, and smelled a whole lot better.

Colt felt the movie theatre beckon. The little guy became fidgety and anxious. Lunch was hurried.

They walked down and across the street to the small theatre across from the backside of the courthouse. It was not like the gargantuan multi-screen Cineplex's in the bigger cities, just a small building sandwiched between Nadine's Dress Shop and the Super Discount Shoe Store on the square. The overhead marquee was small but gaily lighted with blue, red and white neon lights that flickered and hummed. Bright white ones blinked in a circle around the poster of the spotlight feature. The tiny ticket window, facing the sidewalk, was ringed in bulbs that were far too bright, giving the appearance of looking into a dressing room mirror. The smell of popcorn fanned on warmer air in their direction with each swing of the double doors next to it.

It was not unusual, in Green Meadow, to see unchaperoned children and teenagers of all ages on Saturday afternoons at the movies. Trust was another one of those precious and rare things held over from a different era and still existed in this small corner of the world. But, Pop knew that that level of trust would erode fast if there ever should come a time an influx of strangers came to town, jobs at a new factory perhaps, or some other industry.

Stepping inside, Pop saw only two other adults in the theatre. They found the perfect seats, dead center in the auditorium. They sat and settled in, popcorn and sodas in hand. The movie was about to begin. It was noisy, but Colt did not seem to notice, and Pop did not mind it. The animated feature was of little interest to anyone above the age of ten. Colt's contribution to the racket was a running commentary on the movie—his editorial spin on what was happening and his best guesses on what would happen next.

Pop pretended to listen with interest, complete with facial expressions to match. Colt quickly consumed a large soda and excused himself to the restroom half an hour into the movie.

After five minutes, Pop looked nervously back toward the double doors up the aisle that led into the lobby. He became concerned. Colt had had plenty of time to take care of that little bit of business. He should have been back in his seat. He rose and walked up the aisle through the dark auditorium to the swinging door at the rear exit into the brighter, but still dim lighting of the lobby, and then on to the restroom. As he approached the door marked MEN, Pop heard a commotion. A crying teenaged boy shot past him with blood streaming from his nose. He threw the door open in time to hear, "You're not going say a goddamned thing to anyone about this! Ya hear?"

Pop hurried around the tiled partition to see a shabbily dressed boy, seventeen, maybe eighteen, holding Colt by the shirt off the floor against the wall. Terrified, Colt cried.

Pop was shorter and much lighter than the teenager. That didn't matter. "Put the boy down and back away, son," he said calmly and deliberately, steely-eyed.

The boy jerked an angry look toward Pop, still holding Colt off the floor. After tense seconds, he reluctantly dropped Colt. Then flashed a devilish grin at Pop. "I don't think I like you telling me what the hell to do, you old sonofabitch," he hissed, reaching into the pocket of his dirty jeans, clearly too big for him and gathered at the waist by a belt that was equally too long. The end of it hung down over his crotch. He produced a lock-blade hunting knife, as Colt cowered in the corner and cried.

He advanced on Pop, as if stalking him.

Pop did not move, did not change his expression whatsoever. He spent too many years surviving on the streets of Chicago to let a teenager with a bad attitude scare him. Honed instincts of self-preservation swept over him and Pop was no longer in that theatre, in a small town, in north Texas. He was catapulted back to another time, fighting for his life in a back alley of inner city Chicago.

"I'm going to gut you...you bastard," the boy snarled as he lunged at Pop.   Pop stood his ground, intercepting the knife wielding hand at the wrist. It was a quick, smooth motion that twisted the boy's arm behind him.

Pop jerked the arm upward. The boy yelped in pain. While the hoodlum was off-balance, Pop threw him face-first into the restroom wall.

The sound of flesh and bone hitting tile made a sickening thud. The knife fell to the floor with a clank.

With a free hand, Pop picked it up and held it to the now-frightened teenager's throat. "If you want to continue this, then I'll cut your balls off and flush them down the toilet. Or," he added in a quieter, fatherly way, "I can keep your knife and you can develop a better attitude and be nicer to people."

Squirming and whimpering, the boy fought against the old man's grip.

"Your choice," Pop said.

The teenager tried yet again to free himself from the old man's clutches. "Well, what'll it be?" Pop demanded.

He twisted the arm until he heard the cartilage grind in the boy's shoulder. "Okay, okay! Goddamnit! Let me go!"

"One last thing, what's your name?"

One final arm twist and the boy blurted, "Bart Ledbetter."

"Well, young Mr. Ledbetter, I don't think I ever want to see you again," Pop said, shoving him stumbling toward the door. "Now, go crawl back into that stench-filled shit hole you crawled out of…wherever that might be."

Flipping the lid on the trash container, he dropped the knife in it. Only then did Pop become aware he was not alone, or in a Chicago alley. He looked around. Colt sat in a corner, his knees pulled to his chest, creating a tight, tiny human ball.

Pop backed up to the wall and slid down to the floor to sit beside the terrified child. Emulating his young friend's sitting style, Pop studied the boy's face then turned away and let his head rest against the tiled surface behind them. He looked straight ahead. "I bet you didn't expect to have this much excitement today," he said in a near-whisper. "Did ya, Colt?"

"U-uh. No sir." The child sobbed.

"Well, I can't say I'm very proud of how I handled that situation," Pop told him. "I lost my temper. I shouldn't have. And, I certainly shouldn't've been talking like that in front of you." He looked down at Colt. Forgive me?"

Colt nodded. "Uh-huh."

"You know," the old man said, "I don't think your daddy would approve of how I took care of this situation. Do you?"

"Maybe. I dunno."

"I don't know either, but I feel it best he not know about this. What do you think, boy?"

Colt threw his arms around the old man's neck and hugged hard, still sniffling. "I have two secrets to keep, one for Momma and one for you." He paused, and then added, "But we better not make this a *trishun*."

"The word is tradition." He smoothed the boy's hair down and added with a smile, "You're right. This certainly would *not* make a good one." Pop drew a deep breath. "Not at all."

NINE

The new calf born in the fall was an unhealthy runt that would never have any market value, even if it survived. And that was highly unlikely. The tiny bovine had gnarled legs and bulging eyeballs. Since it was too weak to turn out onto pasture with the mother cow, it was kept penned and hand-fed. It was necessary if the animal were to have even a shred of hope. Its destiny and life span were preordained.

Colt intervened when he overheard his father tell his mother it was time to dispose of it. "Feed cost for the little creature just can't be justified."

"But, Daddy," Colt argued, "I don't have a dog and that's a huge food savings right there. Please, Daddy, can I keep him?" He protested, saying he'd take responsibility for keeping the calf fed if his daddy would continue to purchase the feed ration. The numerous cats that prowled the barn were excluded from the *pet* debate, because they were kept only to keep the rodent and bird population under control. They were nearly wild and unapproachable anyway, and could not be considered pets.

Tom made several half-hearted attempts to argue his position, eventually giving in. But, only because he knew that the calf would not live long. He rationalized that it might be a good life-lesson for Colt to take care of it. Although he had concern how the little guy would handle the situation when the calf died, as it inevitably would.

December faded into January. The plains of Texas enjoyed precious few mild days since the first blue northern skated down from Canada in the fall. Bitter cold settled in, and if it wasn't snowing, it threatened to. Temperatures sank into the teens and stayed there, round the clock, for over a week.

Colt woke early on a dark snowy morning to the sound of a cow bawling. He sat up and rubbed sleep from his eyes. Throwing off the cozy, but weighty, layers of blankets, he swung his feet over the edge of the bed to go investigate. His first steps were unsteady on the cold hardwood floor, as he groggily searched for his slippers and robe.

As he passed the television set in the living room, the glowing readout of a digital clock on its top showed 4:47 a.m. He quickened his step through the darkened house to the back door. Yanking back the noisy metal blinds covering the door window, he peered into the darkness, trying to see what the commotion was all about. Unable to, he opened the door for a better look, and his first metallic taste of the cold morning air took his breath.

Once his eyes adjusted, he saw the old mother cow pressing hard against the fence. She bellowed in the direction of the covered shed and pen where Colt kept Butch, the name he'd given the runt calf, because its distorted face resembled a cartoon bulldog he'd seen, once upon a time. Realizing the cow was Butch's mother; it was only natural to assume the calf was in trouble. Slinging open the screen door, he shot out toward the pen and, behind him, the screen door slammed with a loud smack, loud enough to rouse everyone. Running as fast as his little legs would carry him, he paid no attention to the numbing temperatures, his focus was entirely on the pen, as the snow crunched beneath his slippers.

It was calm and the snow was like ornate confetti drifting lazily, in no hurry to make it to the ground, coating the frozen earth to a depth of about three inches, but drifts of a couple of feet piled against vertical structures.

Colt fumbled with the latch on the gate, his fingers and toes numbed and stiffened with the freezing temperatures. Once inside, he ran into the small, protective area to find Butch dead and frozen nearly solid. Falling into ankle-deep hay, he hugged the frost-covered body and cried.

"You did everything you could, son," his father said, coming to stand over him. "His life was much better in the short time he had, because of you." He draped a blanket over Colt's shoulders, lifting him away from the dead animal. Looking up with teary eyes, he saw his mother and father quietly allowing him to mourn.

"Why do living things die, Pop?"

The question broke the silence on an otherwise quiet trip to school. Colt stared at his feet, wiggling his cold toes inside his shoes, holding them close to the warm air of the car's heater.

Pop didn't want to tackle the subject. This was something he thought best left to a parent. Undeterred by the silence, Colt pressed on. "I don't understand why God would make perfectly good people and animals then—poof, let them die. It *must* be God makin' it happen, because no one actually wants to die."

He turned toward the old man, waiting. "Nobody wants to die. Do they Pop?"

The question struck a sensitive nerve that made the hair stand out on the back of Pop's neck. Just a few short weeks before he had seen death as a viable alternative to his private hell and still remained uncertain to the point of keeping the means to accomplish his demise in a drawer beside his bed. Suddenly, he felt compelled to address the lad's questions. "Boy, nobody *wants* to die," he said, "but there are times when living becomes so empty and pointless that dying can simply be an end to the agony." Pop did not need a response from the boy to see the question in his eyes. "Look, Colt. There's more to life than merely breathing and existing. For life to be truly worth living, it should have meaning."

Colt stared at Pop, head tilted. The boy's young life was still a wondrous journey of discovery and learning. That comment simply did not compute. "So. When things happen to me I don't like, that makes me *empty*," the child said, mulling the new information, "and if I can't make all the bad stuff stop, then that makes life *pointless*. Then, when life is empty *and* pointless, killing myself is okay? Right?" He sported a faint smile and looked to Pop for a response, certain he had nailed a profoundly correct response.

Pop's shock could not have been more intense. His heart fluttered and blood rushed to his face. That was the only profound thing at the moment. "No, that's not okay at all!" he said, "And don't ever...*ever* talk like that again. Do you hear me? You can't..."

Colt recoiled at the sudden outburst. Pop snapped his jaws shut abruptly. He stopped talking when he realized he frightened the boy. In a gentler tone, "Look, human beings crave interaction with other human beings. We need friends and family. Without human closeness, people can become disconnected and lonely. Whether we admit it to ourselves or not, we live and thrive on human contact. When we have people in our lives to interact with and to..."

"And to what, Pop?"

"...And to love," Pop said, struggling to get the word out. "Then we'll always have a reason to live long, productive lives."

Colt nodded and appeared to understand. He thought on it. "I'm sure glad I have Momma, Daddy and you then." Reassured, he went on to chatter happily about other things.

But Pop's mind was stuck and only heard the boy as a drone in the distance. He was stupefied, forced to face his own situation, a strong lesson learned, taught him by a six-year-old boy.

TEN

There was no relief from the dreary cold. Skies seldom cleared through the month of January. Daily rituals on the farm were routine and monotonous. Prolonged confinement each day caused patience to thin. Nerves stretched taut, tempers flared. A break in the cycle was needed, an entertaining diversion that positively altered prevailing moods.

An annually anticipated event for a community the cozy size of Green Meadow was at the high school. A winter carnival in the gymnasium was planned for a Saturday night late in the month. It was a well-timed event put on by the senior class to raise funds for an end-of-school class trip after graduation. The carnival worked on several levels, not the least of which was fund-raising.

More importantly for the Bradshaw family, it was the ideal way to get out for an evening, a deserved break from the tedium of daily life. Every year, the timing was just right. The whole family looked forward to it with eager anticipation. Since learning of it, Pop looked forward to it, too, but for a different reason. For him, it would be a quiet evening alone, away from the family for a short time.

Colt was not about to let that happen. On the evening the plan to attend was made, the youngster burst into Pop's bedroom, with no warning, jumped onto the bed, chattering excitedly about all the fun it would be.

Pop sat quietly nearby in a wingback chair, holding a magazine. The old man watched and listened without comment. He allowed the boy to get it all out. Finally, he said, "You guys go on and enjoy yourselves. I'll stay home that night and watch the house."

"Watch the house? What does that mean? You already know what it looks like." Pop tried not to smile. He failed. He then hesitatingly shifted his gaze back to the magazine and said no more.

"Aw, come on Pop," Colt said, pleading, "You can't stay home. It'll be great fun and I wouldn't have as much fun without you."

Mildly irritated, Pop dropped the magazine into his lap. "Now Colt, that should be a time for family...just family."

"Yeah. I know. So why don't you want to go?"

For the first time, Pop realized that Colt thought of him as part of the family, without hesitation or reservation. Suddenly he was overcome and speechless. "I...well, it's like..." contemplating his next comment carefully, Pop studied Colt's face for a moment, chewing the inside of his cheek, mulling a response that might pacify the boy and serve his needs as well.

"Whaddaya think, Pop?"

Finally, with no emotional display, whatsoever, Pop tossed his magazine aside on a nearby table. "I think I'd better brush up on my ring tossing, dart throwing and baseball hurling skills," he said. The plan was set and, now, Pop was part of that plan.

**

The high school gymnasium was large for a school the size of Green Meadow. School tax dollars had been spent wisely. The structure doubled as a community center, often the focal point for such events. The only other venues happened to be churches, but those had a tendency to splinter folks according to faith, Methodist, Baptist, and so on. So the high school gymnasium was the perfect place to pull them all together in the same place for a good time.

Tonight the enclosure was filled with rows of temporary booths partitioned by burlap bagging donated by the local gin, offering games of chance. The aisles were crowded. People waited in short lines by each booth. The expansive domed roof echoed sound easily, reverberating throughout the cavernous room. People laughed. Kids squealed. It all created a roar difficult to speak over. But, it was not unpleasant. It just added to the merriment. Sounds of joy echoed in all directions. The

70

heady aroma of foods mixed in the air from the small concession stand. Popcorn popped, cotton candy spun and long full ears of corn bobbed in boiling water next to a small trough of real butter. The atmosphere was festive.

Colt tried to keep his momma, daddy and Pop close behind him as he hurried from booth to booth. If one lagged behind, the boy grabbed a hand and pulled them along, shouting, "Come on, come on."

A friend of Marge's caused the first defection in the ranks. The two women peeled off, disappearing into the crowd talking of recipes, shopping and such, heading for a classroom outside and down the hall from the gymnasium. It was the room the cake-walk had been set up in. It was much quieter, allowing some good old-fashioned country conversation between neighbors.

Tom and Pop stood behind Colt, as the little guy tried his level best to knock over three leaded milk bottles with a lighter than regulation baseball, as Bobby Joe Peeler walked up behind Tom and slapped him on the shoulder.

Bobby Joe and his family lived in the neighboring community of Red Flats, about ten miles west of Green Meadow. Tom last saw him just before harvest began in the fall, so it was a happy reunion with plenty of news to catch up on. The two gabbed about poor cotton prices and debated ways to make it fetch more. They argued prospects for changing farm subsidies and the high price of farm implements. "Come on Tom," Bobby Joe said, "let me buy you a hotdog."

Tom grinned, patted his bulging belly then frowned and shook his head no. Bobby Joe shrugged. "Okay then. How about just a cup of coffee?"

Tom looked back at Pop and nodded toward Colt who still threw baseballs at bottles, not paying them any mind. Pop gave the okay sign then waved Tom on, meaning he would keep an eye on the boy.

The evening progressed at a lively pace. Even Pop loosened up. He took his chance at several of the booths and won a small clock-radio tossing rings onto soda bottles. He gave it to Colt. The boy beamed with pride and clutched it to his chest, as if he were afraid someone might snatch it from his grasp. He was proud of it and had already vowed to Pop that he would keep it beside his bed forever. It had little monetary value but, to a six-year old, it just as well have been a twenty-four karat gold bar. He proudly told anyone interested, his best friend Pop had won it just for him.

Pop looked down at Colt and put his mouth close to the boy's ear to be heard over the cacophony in the gymnasium. "Come on boy. I have to use the restroom and I can't leave you alone." The two negotiated their way through the throng to the doors leading to the long hall in the main part of the high school. That side of the building was not being used for any part of the carnival. The corridor was poorly lighted and, for the most part, void of people, except for three men talking and passing around a bottle in a brown paper sack. They created their own raucous good time that had nothing to do with the family atmosphere in the next room. The old man and boy approached but could not hear exactly what was said yet, but curse words became the first distinguishable sounds on up inflections. Even before he and Colt made it as far down as where they stood, Pop became uneasy about them.

Pop reached for and held Colt's hand. They walked by the boisterous threesome when one of them suddenly broke into laughter over something said and stumbled backwards into Pop, spewing his sour breath on the smaller old man. "Watch where you're going, you sonofabitch!" He bellowed drunkenly.

Pop squared his shoulders and pushed himself away from the stinking giant who towered over him. He was bald with a bushy fringe, crooked yellowing teeth and wore patched bib overalls with a belly that did not give a wrinkle a chance in the well-worn attire. He was angered by Pop's push-off. "Keep your goddamned hands off me!" he shouted.

"Sir, you really shouldn't be talking like that around a youngster," Pop said in a low voice. "Why don't you just call it a night and…" He stopped short. There was something familiar about the man. "Your last name wouldn't happen to be Ledbetter. Would it?"

The hulk, swaying right to left then back, head hanging loosely upon his shoulders, stared for a moment through liquor soaked eyes. Then started wagging a finger at Pop. "Now I know who you are. You're the bastard who stole my boy's huntin' knife."

"No," said Pop, "I'm the bastard who taught your boy not to pull a knife on strangers. He gave it to me willingly."

Colt started tugging on Pop's arm, but the old man did not yield or break eye contact. Ledbetter ground his teeth and growled, "I think I'm just gonna whip the crap out of you here and now."

As he attempted to lunge at Pop, his two companions decided it was time to intervene. Moving in on each side of him, they grabbed his arms. "Come on Burton," one of them said. "Why do you have to be such an ornery drunk? This little piss-ant ain't worth the effort."

"This ain't over," Ledbetter roared, shaking a fist at Pop as his companions pulled him away. "Watch your back. I'll getcha. Ya hear me, you sonofabitch! I *will* getcha!"

Pop watched them go, unmoving, even though Colt pulled at his hand, trying to open his fist. He had to stay prepared, not knowing yet if the animal impulse that drove that man might kick in then tear loose from his friends and come after him. But, the farther Ledbetter moved away, the more relaxed Pop became. He reluctantly resumed his quest for the restroom, pausing now and then, to look over his shoulder. Pop saw that Ledbetter, even drunk, meant what he said; that he would come after him. Pop figured that a morally bankrupt man as that could do great bodily harm with no remorse. Pop felt so much misplaced anger coming from that man, he had to take him seriously.

Colt clutched his radio tightly in one hand, squeezing Pop's hand in the other, shaken and frightened. Pop noticed. Dropping to a knee, the old man looked him in the eye. "Boy, everything'll be fine," he said. "You just can't give in to a bully, or they'll hound you forever after."

Colt nodded, but uncertainty shaded the lad's positive response. "Do you understand what I'm saying?" Pop asked.

"I guess so," Colt said, nodding again.

The two resumed their trip into the restroom. While Colt waited, Pop washed his hands. Suddenly, the restroom door swung open and slammed into the wall, shattering the silence, so startling Colt, he stumbled and fell.

There stood Burton Ledbetter without his companions. "I've decided that radio the boy's holdin' is a good trade for the huntin' knife you stole."

Pop continued washing his hands. "What is it about restrooms and the Ledbetter family? Do you fellas just enjoy the atmosphere? Maybe the smell reminds you of home. Is that it?"

Pop calmly rolled off a paper towel and directed his attention to Colt. "Are you okay, boy?" Colt nodded and got back on his feet wrapping up his radio with both arms, turning away so his prize was out of sight. He had no intention of letting it go.

"What do you think we ought to do about this situation, boy?" the old man asked, as if they were alone, looking at his own reflection in the mirror above the sink.

Pop's calmness in the face of adversity and being talked to like an adult gave Colt courage. He puffed out his chest and said, "You're right, Pop. He *is* a bully. Someone ought to kick the crap out of him." Pop shot him an incredulous look. At the same time Ledbetter made a move toward Colt to take the radio.

Once the dirty drunk's attention shifted, Pop picked up the trashcan and smashed the lumbering hulk with all his might in back of the head. It dazed him. He stumbled down to his knees. But he was still conscious.

"Oh, no," Pop whispered, as Ledbetter pulled himself to his feet. He turned to Colt. "Get out of here! Run!"

Colt scampered and skated around the partition slipping on the slick tile floor and disappeared through the door. Pop advanced on the man, trying to maintain the advantage. A right cross into Ledbetter's temple barely even caused his head to bobble.

The only thing he accomplished was a sharp pain in his knuckles that numbed his whole fist. Pop grimaced, shaking his hand trying to regain pain-free feeling in it. He realized he might as well have slammed his fist into the wall.

Straightening his back to boast his full six-foot-five frame, Ledbetter smiled to let Pop know the blow did more damage to his hand than the big man's face. He moved on Pop and swung wildly.

Pop tried to duck but was caught with a glancing blow to the top of the head. It was enough. It sent him reeling. He lost sure footing and stumbled into a stall. He fell in a sitting position onto a toilet. "I'm getting far too old for this," he growled through gritted teeth.

Ledbetter awkwardly reached in to grab him by the collar. Pop kicked him hard between the legs. Exhaling violently, the rank smelling behemoth roared like a bear. He careened backwards holding his crotch with both hands and fell between two sinks attached to the wall.

Pop was on him before he hit the floor, trashcan in hand, beating him repeatedly, as the drunken farmer groaned and finally lay motionless. Breathing hard, trashcan overhead, he waited, not wanting to move in case Ledbetter were still conscious and wanted to continue the fray. Pop knew he could not keep this up much longer if he did.

Eventually, Pop staggered away from the big man and tossed the waste container aside. It clanked across the floor. He stepped back with his hands on his hips. He sucked air into his lungs then bent at the waist, trying to regain his breath.

Then he noticed Colt peeking around the door, apparently having witnessed the entire altercation. Pop wiped the sweat from his forehead. "I know there must be a better way to handle these situations," he said then took a breath with a loud wheeze, "but darned if I know what that is." He touched the growing knot on his forehead. "I suppose it'd be best if your momma and daddy didn't know about this either."

Colt rolled his eyes. "Here we go again."

"By the way, what do you mean, 'kick the crap out of him'?" Pop said. "You're not supposed to be talking like that."

"I thought it needed sayin' and that was the right time to say it," Colt said, turning to leave. "It sure got the job done." He hugged his radio tighter yet.

ELEVEN

"I could call the Sheriff's office and have Barry Brown out here in a few minutes. That is, if you want to file a complaint against Ledbetter. And, I strongly suggest you do." Tom sat across from Pop at the kitchen table while Marge filled a plastic bag with ice for the old man to hold to his swelling forehead. The bruise darkened.

Colt stood by Pop's chair, nudging him gently with his little shoulder. "I'm sorry for tellin'," he said. "I didn't know what else to say when Daddy asked me."

"That's enough Colt," Tom said.

Patting the little guy's back, Pop said, "It's okay, boy. You did the right thing. You told the truth." He then fingered the lump on his forehead. "Besides, it would have been difficult concealing this large purple knot." Pop thought on the situation for a moment. "No, I don't see any need to file a complaint. The man was slobbering drunk and probably wouldn't have behaved that way sober. Sometimes a man will do crazy things when he's been drinking."

Tom didn't understand the old man's defense of such a scoundrel. "I'm not so sure about that," he said in a measured response. "The Ledbetter's have a reputation for meanness and dishonesty. He really should be held accountable. Shoot, even the old lady, Irma Ledbetter, was thrown in jail for assault once. She hit a cashier at the grocery store in the head with a can of peas. For heaven sakes, the girl was just a high-schooler working part-time. Mrs. Ledbetter accused the poor thing of purposely ringing up the wrong price. When the girl politely protested...ka-wham!" Tom slammed a fist into his open palm for emphasis. "The old sot grabbed a can and hit her across the face with it. It left a nasty, bloody bruise...and a permanent scar, for Christ's sake. Can you believe any sane person would do something like that over six cents?"

Although she sat without speaking at the end of the table, Marge quietly nodded with raised eyebrows, in agreement with everything her husband said.

The old man considered the suggestion momentarily. "Even so," Pop said, "I think it best to leave it be." He harbored feelings from another place and another time where laws governing the general public did not apply to a subculture to which he belonged. The only laws at that time had been those coming from a personal sense of right and wrong and ones' willingness to enforce them. As a consequence, he spent years trying to avoid law enforcement. No matter what the offense, people in Pop's situation were suspected first and often made scapegoats for crimes not easily solved.

Tom and Marge Bradshaw could not understand Pop's thinking but respect ran deep for his sense of fairness. They didn't press the issue further, since Colt had not been harmed and the old guy had put himself at risk to protect him. For that alone, he deserved to have his wishes granted.

While the three adults continued talking about the incident, Colt slipped off and headed for his bedroom. The fun, together with the trauma that capped the evening, exhausted him. He needed no prodding to go to bed. Slipping into flannel pajamas, he walked to the window in his bedroom and looked up at the fingernail moon shining brightly in the clear night sky. Shuddering slightly from the cold radiating through the glass, he gazed upon the twinkling stars and passing cloud wisps while standing as a tiny soldier at attention, fingers laced together behind him.

"Good night Mr. Moon," he whispered, "and thank you for Pop…my friend."

**

February began with a hint of approaching spring in the air. It was still cold but the warm sun made headway, piercing the chill. Winter was in the earliest stages of losing its strangle hold on the Texas plains.

After breakfast one Sunday, Colt volunteered to feed the cows. Of course, he naturally assumed Pop would come along and help.

Although the sun hinted warmth, even the smallest breeze was enough reason to wear heavy coats zipped to the top, plus warm gloves, as Pop and Colt walked out into the frigid morning, directly into the rising sun. Playing with his breathing, Colt created little frosty clouds, imitating a locomotive. As he did, he became inquisitive. It was his nature. "Pop, where would you be right now if you weren't living with us?"

"Oh, probably a warmer climate somewhere," he said. "I couldn't take this cold all day and all night. He could not hide discomfort with the question or his answer, thinking about what might have happened should things have gone only slightly different. He did not really want to discuss it at all, so, he chose to keep his answer short, without detail. "I would have preferred warmer weather if I found myself without a place to stay some nights."

"Why don't you get a place of your own and just stay in one place?" he asked, confused by the concept of homelessness. Colt's eyes peered from under the woolen cap, having to tilt his head far back just to see up into Pop's face.

Pop threw open the aromatic cedar cross-buck door of the hay bin and stepped inside. Two mice, startled by the sudden flood of daylight, scurried for safer haven within the spacious corner of the barn that housed the neatly stacked bales of hay. The sweet smell of alfalfa filled the air.

Since Colt treaded into conversational territory Pop did not care to talk about, he changed the subject. "You know, it looks like we'll have plenty of hay to tide those cows over until good grazing grass in the pasture comes out in a few weeks and starts growing."

"Why would *anybody* want to move around like that?" Colt persisted. He took on his determined pose; hands on hips and legs spread. "Movin' around all over the darned place and never havin' friends...gosh...that can't be any fun. Can it?" Colt sat on a bale of hay. He rubbed his numbed cheeks.

"Wouldn't it be nice to have a place that's warm and safe all the time?"

Pop became annoyed with the barrage of questions and more than a little nervous about being put in a situation he might have to lie. "Here boy," he said, tinged with sharpness, as he grabbed a bale by its wire binding. He tossed it. It dropped in front of Colt. "Drag this to the pen." He threw his head to one side in the direction of the livestock enclosure. "I'll be right behind you with another one."

The bale was heavy. Pop knew it might be too much for the boy. But, he believed it would distract the overly inquisitive youth, maybe even to the point of forgetting the uncomfortable questions he did not want to answer. Sure enough, it taxed the limit of Colt's strength but he struggled without complaint. Not wanting to disappoint Pop, he grimaced, groaned, growled and tugged with all his might. With every snort of white from his nostrils, he inched closer to his goal. The distance was no more than fifty feet, but for a lad of less than seventy pounds, it might as well have been a quarter mile. The exertion turned his nose and cheeks bright red.

Having made the trip with his bale quickly, Pop cut the wire and spread the compacted leafy feed over a large area, releasing its sweet pungent smell. The cows nudged Pop out of the way to eat. The old man glanced back at his little friend who had not made it halfway yet and started toward him to help. Thinking on it, he decided against it. Taking off his gloves and shoving them into his hip pocket, he folded his arms, leaned against the pen and waited.

Several minutes passed before Colt succeeded in dragging the heavy bale of hay all the way with no assistance. Trickles of sweat dotted his temples despite the cold morning air. He panted like a puppy dog. "Here it is," he said between gasps, sitting down heavily on the bale.

Fighting his urge to express admiration, Pop avoided eye contact. "You did good boy," he mumbled, figuring any display of excitement would be tantamount to an invitation to resume the interrogation.

Pop underestimated Colt's resolve to get answers. Before the little guy had even caught his breath, the questions resumed. "Why do you want to move around so much? Why do you always want to go someplace else? Do you think things will be better? I don't understand."

Pop pulled the bale from under Colt, forcing him to stand, and snipped the wire. "We're going to need one more bale," he said, tossing the hay in an area away from the hovering cows.

"Do you like living alone?"

Pop spun around to face the boy. "You're not going to quit asking questions, are you?" Colt rocked heel to toe, then back again with a shy smile. "I'll tell you what," Pop said, "if you'll fetch another bale of hay, snip the binding and spread it over there, then I'll answer some of your questions." He believed he had just offered a six-year-old a fool's bet, one he could not lose, ultimately shutting down the well-oiled little question machine.

Colt rolled his eyes. He sighed. "Okay," he said with an exaggerated drawl. Turning away, he marched with renewed sense of purpose back to the barn. His curiosity was a more powerful motivator than his physical deficiency was a deterrent.

Pop shot a quick glance of disbelief toward heaven. The little guy appeared to be marching in cadence to music only he could hear. Taking a position atop a large fence post anchoring the corral, Pop sat and watched, merrily swinging his crossed ankles, sporting a crooked grin, supremely confident he would be answering no more questions. Nonetheless, his admiration for Colt jumped another notch in that moment—if that was even possible.

The struggle seemed endless for the small boy. After five minutes, he remained a formidable distance from his goal. Each time he paused to rest and Pop offered to help, Colt got up and began tugging all over again. He marveled at the kid's pluck. He knew Colt was an especially intelligent child but, until now, he had not realized the tiny man's dedication to a cause.

Eventually Colt made it. Pop climbed down and joined him by the bale. The boy fell over on top of it exhausted. "That's good enough," Pop said, taking the wire-cutting pliers from his pocket. "You did well."

Colt sat bolt upright, huffing. "No," he said, taking the cutters from Pop, "we made a deal." Tiny hands wrestled with the cumbersome cutters but eventually severed both wires holding the bale intact, and Colt spread the hay in the promised area.

"Well," Pop said scratching his forehead, "I suppose I owe you some answers." He did not even try to hide the admiration beaming in his smile. He took a couple of quick steps toward the house and added, "And maybe a cup of hot cocoa, too." Colt fell in behind Pop matching his step, strutting with pride, eagerly anticipating hot cocoa and answers.

Tom had gone into Green Meadow to check cotton and grain prices. He had not sold the entire crop at harvest and considered selling more, maybe all of it, if the prices were better. It was always an intense guessing game of market prices versus storage costs.

Marge sat in a sunny corner of her bedroom at the sewing machine, totally engrossed in the artistry of making a new dress. She had had trouble finding enough clothes to wear since losing the weight from her heart attack. Since that time, she vowed to stay thin for appearance, as well as future health. She believed a new wardrobe would be the perfect incentive. She felt good and she looked good. And she knew it. That prompted her to begin a campaign of getting Tom to lose weight, too.

Pop and Colt shed the heavy outer clothing at the backdoor. The old man immediately began taking care of his part of the bargain by pouring milk in a pot, setting it on the stove and dumping a healthy amount of powdered cocoa and sugar in it. He then sat at the table in the kitchen, "Come on over here and sit down, boy."

Colt complied without hesitation, looking eagerly to Pop. "Okay," Pop said, "Ask your questions."

Colt rocked in his seat with excitement. "Have you *always* been without a real home?"

"No."

"Don't you want a real home?"

"No."

Colt fell forward resting his head on his palms. "I don't understand."

Pop shrugged. "I'm not sure I do either." After a brief, uncomfortable silence the old man continued, "Look, maybe if I asked you something, it would make things clearer for you." He toyed with a sugar bowl as a focal point while he thought over the best way to tell his story. "Let's say that, without warning, one morning you woke up and discovered something really bad had happened to your momma and daddy and they were no longer around. How would you feel?"

"I guess I'd be really, really sad." Colt frowned, shifting in his seat, nervous.

"That's right," Pop said, "and would this house be the same as it was before the bad thing happened?"

Colt scratched his head. "Well, no. It'd be empty."

Pop seized that opportunity. "That's right, it *would* be empty. But it wouldn't just be empty of people but, also, empty of love and empty of laughter and empty of...well, everything that makes it a home. Then, Colt, you'd become empty, too." He reached across and placed a finger on the little man's heart. "Right here. You'd be empty, right here." He tapped Colt's chest one more time to drive home the point. "It would just be a house, a building, nothing more. A home is forever, but a house is... well, let's just say a person can sleep anywhere."

Colt assumed a quizzical look as though he were not certain at all he had a handle on where Pop was going with the discourse. "Houses are not the only thing that can become empty," Pop added, walking to the stove, "people can become empty, too." Returning to Colt's side of the table, he poured a steaming mug full. "Okay?"

"Okay." He frowned. I guess."

Pop squatted, sitting on his heels, looking the boy squarely in the face. "Colt, no matter where a man chooses to stay, or just sleep for the night," he said, placing his finger on the boy's heart, "this is home." Pop saw the light in Colt's eyes.

TWELVE

A late winter rain dampened barren fields across Bentley County. The weather warmed, freezing temperatures no longer a serious threat. The smell of freshly turned, wet earth filled the air. Fields remained void of crops but were being prepared for planting in the next few weeks. The fresh, earthy smell was like expensive perfume to a farmer.

The air, in no way, could be described as sweet at the Ledbetter farm, since it carried the nauseating stench of sodden and neglected hog pens. A casual inspection would reveal an overgrown yard around the house, as well as bare trees and bushes which, once warmer weather set in, would transform into a veritable jungle hiding all but the roof of the dilapidated house. The yard was littered with discarded kitchen appliances and car parts, some dating back to the Second World War. And this picture could not be complete without the old sofa on the front porch that set like a beached whale. To the uninitiated, the property could easily be mistaken for abandoned.

Farther back, beyond the house, was no better. The junk simply changed from household items to rusted deteriorating farm implements and tractors. Whatever was around the Ledbetter farm deemed worthless was either hauled out of the house and left or, if they didn't see it as in the way, it stayed exactly where it stopped working. They not only lived there, it was also the family dump ground. It was amazing that a place in such disarray and disrepair could provide a livelihood for a family of five.

Burton and Irma Ledbetter bickered most of every day. Alcoholism plagued them both and that brought on bouts of depression. Living amid squalor added to this white-trash scenario. There did not need to be a reason for an argument. And, it was about the only time they spoke to one another. It was a lifestyle. The hovel the Ledbetter family called home rocked with negative energy.

Bart was the eldest of three children. Kendall was the fourteen year-old brother following the example set by his older brother who, in turn, followed the example set by the old man, Burton. Idiocy had begotten idiocy.

The deviation was twelve-year old Jane, the baby. Neat, clean and well mannered, she earned the respect of her peers at school, yet, was a genetic oddity, given her family situation. A pleasant child, Jane did not go unnoticed by those she came in contact with, but for all the right reasons, unlike the remainder of her family. In need of dental work and already developing the acne problem of a youngster several years her senior, she could not be considered cute. But, those who knew her did not notice these minor imperfections. Her personality beamed, endearing her to everyone. And, also, to everyone she met, it quickly became clear she worked at overcoming the sins of her family. Every conversation that occurred in Green Meadow about the Ledbetters always ended with the phrase *...except for Jane.* She had single-handedly carved a welcomed place for herself in the community.

It was the start of a typical day at the Ledbetter farm; husband and wife trading obscenities over a perceived wrong of some sort, trivial to the point neither would remember it minutes later, possibly could not remember. This would be contingent upon whether they had sobered from the night before.

At the same time, Bart and Kendall bumped heads over whose turn it was to feed the hogs. In venomous tone, "You little bastard," Bart said, "What makes you think you can argue with me?"

Kendall took a step forward. Unafraid and going nose-to-nose, "Just because you're bigger and older," he said, "doesn't mean I can't kick your ass." Bart put the heel of his hand to his brother's forehead and shoved hard enough to make him stumble backwards and fall.

"You sonofabitch!" Kendall shrieked. "Leave me alone goddamnit!"

"Shut up, you little piss ant," Bart said.

Back in the house, hearing the profanity laced argument just outside her bedroom window, on one side, and hearing her mother and father going at it in equally vile manner in the next room, Jane sat, hugging a pillow, legs tucked under her, rocking back a forth in the center of her bed. Body closed off to it all, she prayed hard to have one day—just *one* day, her family could be pleasant.

After the silent prayer, her mind drifted. She had long ago been forced to learn the art of putting herself in another place and another time in order to preserve her already damaged sanity and sense of decency that was on the verge of eroding. Images of distant shores and tropical settings insulated her from foul language that flew through the air like demons seeking to possess. Even at the formative age of twelve, she knew that living in the muck was to eventually become coated with its stench.

Her oldest brother, Bart, was totally disrespectful to his mother and thought nothing of cursing her to her face without provocation. Only fear kept him from treating his father the same way. Instead of showing how scared he was of being beaten by his old man, he took it out on Kendall and Jane in non-stop verbal and physical abuse. He was a threat if he were awake and within close proximity to either of them. That is how frequent it was. Kendall, only fourteen, could not successfully turn his frustration on Bart, so he, too, made Jane's life miserable. Bottom line: Abuse, like raw sewage, flows downhill in such a family. Jane was at the bottom. This was a testament to her strength of character. It was phenomenal.

She found great comfort in going to her private place in the barn, high up in the joists, below the rafters, among the dust and cobwebs. It was a platform built for storage. It always waited, and often lured; a place a little closer to heaven that she called her own. Even as she sat on her bed trying to block out the misery that was her life, she took great comfort in simply the thought of climbing the precarious ladder rungs that had been carelessly nailed to a support post, up, up, up to the musty perch, twenty feet above the dirt floor where she kept books, dolls and assorted toys. All of which helped create an all-important imaginary world. If she was not in school or doing chores around the farm, she usually could be found there. Jane Ledbetter was doing an amazing job of raising herself.

**

"Daddy, since I already ride the school bus home *after* school, don't you think it's about time I started riding it in the mornings, too?" Colt asked, with his finger in the belt loop of Tom's blue jeans, tugging. It was a subtle way of letting his daddy know he wanted an answer before he would let him walk away. Well, whaddaya think, Daddy?" Colt stood as a soldier at attention waiting for the order to stand at ease.

The routine that had been set to drive him to school in the morning had evolved, simply because it allowed extra time for Colt to get ready and eat breakfast. Tom took a couple more turns on a nut that attached one of the points to a chisel plow, as he bent at the waist next to the implement attached to the rear of the tractor. He dropped the wrench on the concrete floor. The echo filled the cavernous barn. He wiped his brow with back of his gloved hand. "The school bus, huh?" He took off the gloves and dropped down, sitting on his heels. He put his hands on Colt's shoulders, eyeing the boy for a moment face to face. Then he smiled. "This is a mighty big step Colt. Are you sure you're ready for it?"

"Oh, yes sir!"

"Then, by golly, the school bus it is, starting tomorrow morning." Tom bounced back to his feet then froze with one caveat on the tip of his finger. "You'll have to be out at the road early to wave it down because the driver isn't accustomed to stopping here. Understand?"

"I'll ask Pop to get me out of bed early. Thanks Daddy. I'm going to tell him right now."

Colt slept little that night, waking often. He was excited about riding the school bus in the morning for the first time. He was nervous about oversleeping, determined to show his parents he could be trusted. When time to get out of bed finally came, he needed no assistance. Bounding to his feet he got ready for school in record time.

Colt stopped at the door of Pop's bedroom where the old guy was making up his bed. "Come on Pop. We have to eat breakfast early so I don't miss the bus."

"Why don't *I* fix you breakfast for a change," his mother said, calling from the kitchen. "I'm feeling much better and, frankly, beginning to miss housework...if you can believe that." She laughed. "Come on Colt. I'll have oatmeal ready in a few minutes."

Pushing thinning hair away from his face, Pop paced one tight circle, clearly a bit lost having that duty taken away. The seasons were not only changing outdoors, but also a change had been clearly set in motion within the house as well.

Colt ate breakfast so quickly he had to be reprimanded several times. He could not control himself, swallowing oatmeal by the spoons-full without chewing. Twice, Colt bolted for the door and had to be detained, once to brush his teeth and, again, to get his backpack. Finally, in a small fit of frustration, "Can I go now? Please?"

Giving Colt's hair one final grooming swipe with her palm, "Sure, Honey. Go on."

Colt threw open the back door and did not let the screen door slow him down, shoving it hard, slamming it into a rocking chair on the back porch. He hollered, "G'bye Daddy. G'bye Pop." He leaped from the three-step porch and disappeared around the corner of the house.

Marge caught the screen door before it slammed shut and stepped out onto the porch. With stealth, she stepped off of it and peered around the edge of the house to watch Colt. Tom joined her in peeking around the corner of the house. Colt occasionally broke into a trot, up the driveway, toward the road. They watched, arm in arm, as Colt took this next step into boyhood.

Shortly, the bus arrived, old brakes squealing, as it came to an easy stop. The doors popped open. Colt turned and waved, fully aware that his momma and daddy watched. With a rev, grinding gears and assorted squeaks, rattles and squeals the aging bus rolled down the section-line dirt road in a brown cloud of dust.

As he cleared the top step and looked across the crowded bus, Colt's excitement suddenly faded and changed to apprehension. "Take a seat," the bus driver told him. "You can't stand up. It's not allowed."

Kids jammed every seat, squealing and laughing. It was loud and they all seemed to be looking at him. The bus swayed and jerked. He listed side to side, as he attempted to walk down the aisle. He had to steady his advance with both hands. The Bradshaw farm was near the end of the route. The bus was crowded. He kept his head down and walked with reservation, not looking anyone in the eye, trying to find an open seat. Seeing that he was nervous, several of the older kids taunted him. Suddenly, he felt a hand on his arm. He turned, startled, to see a girl about twice his age. Colt thought she was the prettiest thing he had ever seen. He was instantly smitten.

"Why don't you sit with me?" She slid close to the window to make room.

Colt climbed tentatively into the seat and sat near the edge of it as far from her as possible. Embarrassed, yet infatuated, he stole glances. Her beautiful blue eyes and long, board-straight blonde hair had his attention.

She noticed. "Hi, my name is Jane…Jane Ledbetter," she said cheerfully, seeing his discomfort, "And you're Colt Bradshaw. Aren't you?"

Colt snapped full eye contact for the first time. "How do you know who I am?"

"Let's just say I learned a lot about you, your family, and your hired hand the night of the winter carnival in the high school gymnasium," she said with a shrug. Her cheeks flushed. She turned away to look out the window at the bare fields they passed. "I have a feeling a lot of it wasn't true." Her voice sank to a mutter, "Since it was my father saying it."

A look of recognition swept over Colt's face. He did not know how to respond and said nothing.

After a time, she looked back. "Why don't I save you a seat on the bus every morning?" she asked, breaking the uncomfortable silence.

"You betcha! That'd be great." The sparkle in his eyes shifted to high beam. He sat up straight, sporting the broad grin of pride, having discovered a new friend.

**

The weeks that followed were pleasant for Colt, as Jane quickly filled the role of mentor. Every morning he talked over his most recent problems at school. She advised him on the best way to navigate the perilous waters of first grade. The bond was tight from the get-go, becoming stronger everyday.

One afternoon in early spring the two giggled and carried on about this and that, as the bus jerked and swayed on the way home. Since the bus route was reversed in the afternoon, Colt was one of the first to get off.

"Hey, why don't you get off at our house and have supper with us?" Colt suggested. "I'm sure I could get Pop to drive you home before dark."

Jane's smile faded. "I don't think that's a good idea."

"Aw, come on," Colt pleaded, "You'll have fun. I promise."

She said nothing, as a twinge of fear tickled her stomach.

He looked with hopeful eyes. Her face tightened, as a decision tried to surface.

He crossed his heart. "It's no problem. Really."

Jane's girlish sense of wonder took over. In a flash, she was intensely curious about life inside the Bradshaw home— any home, other than the pigsty she was forced to live in. She chewed on her lower lip, wondering what their house looked like. She only knew of life in her own, certain it *had* to be better somewhere else. But, she needed proof. She wanted to know—she desperately wanted to know. "Okay, I'll do it."

The bus stopped at the driveway to Colt's house and the two were off it in a matter of seconds after she made the decision. It happened before she had time to reconsider.

Jane had already experienced one growth spurt. She stood head and shoulders taller than Colt. Her clean, but well-worn, clothing was tight and ill fitting. She pushed down on her pant legs trying to make them appear longer but remained well above her ankles.

Colt took two steps for every one of hers. He rattled on about what they could do for the next couple of hours before supper.

As they approached the house, Jane slowed, beginning to think she may have made a bad decision. Knowing a phone call home to notify her parents was the right thing to do she became queasy. Having to call after already committing scared her. At the same time she was scared not to. A sickening lump swelled in her throat.

Embarrassed over her appearance, Jane stopped at the back door, nervously smoothing her hair, but Colt was not about to let her back out. "Come on in," he said. He snatched up her hand and opened the screened door, gently guiding her through it.

It was a simple house similar to thousands dotting the landscape of farm country. But it was a brand new experience to Jane and the crisp neatness was enough to steal her heart and take her breath. "Oh my," she murmured. It might as well have been the Taj Mahal. Studying every detail, she ran her fingers over tabletops, picture frames and anything else that caught her eye. Everything was neat and orderly, glistening clean. She felt off-balance, as if she might stumble and break something precious. She breathed in the smell. "It's like heaven in here." The sweet smell of potpourri permeated the entire house. It was more than a house; it was a home that exuded peace, tranquility and love and all were only vague concepts to Jane. These were things she had only been made peripherally aware of, through books and television, certainly not from parental guidance.

The sound of the sewing machine hummed intermittently in the back bedroom and a voice wafted from down the hall, "Is that you, Colt?"

"Yeah, it's me, Momma. I have a friend with me, too."

Marge appeared in the living room seconds later, extending her hand to Jane. "Well, hello there. I'm Marge Bradshaw," she said, smiling broadly.

Jane nervously wiped her dampened palms on her jeans then thrust it out to Marge. "Hi. I'm Jane Ledbetter," she stammered.

Two male voices and a slamming back door distracted the three. Within seconds, Tom and Pop appeared. "Well who do we have here?" Tom asked.

With beaming pride, "This is my new friend," Colt said, "Jane Ledbetter."

Pop raised an eyebrow. "Ledbetter, huh?" He could not believe old man Ledbetter would allow his daughter to be here, but said nothing more.

The remainder of the afternoon, Colt showed Jane around the farm and let her help with his reading assignment. During which, she felt at peace in Colt's world. She longed to stay to become part of it.

Following supper, Pop volunteered to drive Jane home, but Tom refused to let him go alone. "Burton Ledbetter is unpredictable, *even sober*," he said, "but if he's been drinking it could get ugly." Tom thought it prudent for Pop to have back up—just in case.

In the pickup cab, little Jane trembled, tears welled in her eyes, because she did not want to leave, afraid her father would be angry.

Tom noticed. "Jane, I want you to know you're welcome at our house any time, and if you ever need anything…or if things just become too much for you, call us. Okay?"

She nodded and squeaked, "Okay."

The sound of the truck driving up the poorly maintained and heavily rutted, muddy driveway brought Burton Ledbetter to the front porch to greet the visitors. But, it was obvious in his face that it would not be a pleasant occasion. "Get the hell out of that truck, girl!" he bellowed, before the pickup had come to a full stop.

Opening the door for Jane, Pop locked eyes with old man Ledbetter, his jaw muscles flexed, fighting an urge to smash the stinking farmer's head with something heavy and hard, quelling a strong desire to go on the offensive.

Tom got out and talked across the hood of the truck. "Now Burton," he said calmly, "Take it easy. I want you to know I have never met a better mannered child. And she—"

"Mind your own goddamned business!" Ledbetter roared, grabbing Jane by the arm, nearly jerking her off her feet.

"I'm sorry," she cried. "I'll never do it again. Please, don't hurt me."

Ledbetter walked away with Jane in-tow. He shouted over his shoulder, "Get the hell off my property! Both of you!"

Taking a couple of steps, Pop made a move to follow. Tom intercepted him. "We'll have to depend on Jane to call us if he gets out of hand," he told the older man, "For now, we'd better stay out of it, or that crotchety old so-and-so will have every right to call the Sheriff on *us*."

Behind closed doors, old man Ledbetter slung Jane onto a nearby chair, hurling one obscenity after another. She cowered, curling her body tight, covering her head. She sobbed. It was a primitive response to an animal-like attack, but it was the only way she knew to handle her father when his anger was like this and out of control.

Irma Ledbetter sat across the room, drunk, beer bottle in hand, watching television. She only occasionally glanced at Burton's verbal assault on Jane, without expression, without interest.

Long after they left the room, Jane sat motionless, fearing a return. Finally, she slowly began uncurling, cautiously making her way to the door. She looked everywhere for her father but hoped she would not see him. All she wanted was to get out of that house undetected and away—away to her special place. Running across the yard, she meandered through the obstacle course of junked washers, refrigerators and car

94

fenders. She heard the distinctive drone of a tractor engine and noticed Bart plowing a field nearby. Kendall walked to the hog pen with a bucket in his hand.

As she ran by him, he grabbed her arm. "So, the old man gave it to ya good, did he?" He spat on the ground in front of her. "Serves you right, you little slut."

Wrenching her arm from his grasp, Jane ran into the barn and hurriedly climbed to the top. She lay down on the platform, high above the ground, her special place, and cried.

But, Kendall was not ready to end his hateful game. To his twisted mind, her pain was an open invitation for fun. He tossed the bucket of slop for the hogs aside and ran into the barn after her. He started climbing the ladder. "The old man didn't whip you but I think I will," he muttered, as if to himself, but loud enough for her to hear.

"Go away and leave me alone," she said without lifting her head.

"Nope. Not until I whack your butt good." He made it near the top, peering over the surface of the platform, like a crocodile surfacing, looking to where she lay. "Now I've gotcha."

Jane jumped to her feet. "Go away and leave me alone!" she shouted, her face crimson and distorted, crying harder yet.

She stepped back. Her brother joined her atop the platform. Kendall picked up one of her books. "I'm going to smack your ass with this book 'til it's numb," he hissed. He stalked her. Taking one more step backwards, she fell, followed by a sickening thud and crack. Then silence.

"Oh no. Oh no. Oh no." Kendall repeated, sliding down the ladder. Immediately after hitting the ground he dropped down beside Jane's twisted body on the dirt floor of the barn.

She wheezed heavily and labored for every breath. "Please. Go away and leave me alone..." Her voice trailed. Those were her last words.

THIRTEEN

Tom leaned sideways. "What do you think, Pop? Was it an accident?" He whispered directly into the old man's ear, eyes fixed on the preacher.

Since hearing of the sad news about Jane Ledbetter, he said little about it, but when asked, he was ready with an opinion. Talking low from the side of his mouth, "Regardless how it actually happened, sir, ol' man Ledbetter should be held entirely accountable because of the way he abused her. Of all the sordid things I've ever seen, the way he treats his own children overshadows it all." He flicked a gum wrapper on the floor with the point of his shoe. "We only saw a small sample of what that poor child went through. I'm sure of that." Straightening, he again gave full attention to the open casket, his sadness profound. The only thing visible of little Jane was her lifeless ash-white facial profile. It bore serenity; something she had not known in life.

The preacher droned on and on about eternity, peace, and heaven, using all the comforting, but well worn, words common to funeral services. He spoke, standing behind the open casket surrounded by cut flower arrangements, making sweeping gestures of piety with a Bible in one hand, punctuating his committed reverence for the occasion.

Pop leaned forward, past Tom, for a clearer view of the Ledbetter family sitting across the aisle and two rows ahead. What he saw disgusted him. It had the same effect as witnessing the aftermath of a train wreck...repulsive, but impossible to look away from. Burton Ledbetter stared out the window, restlessly checking his watch every few seconds. The two boys, Bart and Kendall, jabbed one another, giggling and Irma Ledbetter was drunk, eyes glazed. She was in a stupor.

Pop fell back against the pew and ground his teeth. To lose a precious child and show no more remorse than that nauseated him. His mind reeled to a different time—a time

97

when he suddenly lost those dearest to him without warning and the crippling pain that haunted him. He could not hold back tears that escaped his eyes and trickled down his cheeks. He let them be and let them track, an open display of his affection for a little girl who deserved at least that. Jane Ledbetter deserved tears as much as she deserved happiness in life but never knew—a child discarded.

**

Colt cried, off and on, since he found out about his best friend three days before. The news had come as a blow when his momma and daddy first sat him down and attempted to make him understand. But his child's mind worked overtime at building a wall, one tall enough and strong enough to keep him in denial. The only death he had experienced was the calf he coddled and nursed, but never a friend, a girl he idolized and believed God had created just to be his lifelong pal. He refused to believe he would never see her again and, therefore, did not give it any room in his mind. His mourning was more like missing a friend that moved out of town, but he knew—just knew, in his juvenile mind, it would be a temporary separation. He looked upon Jane's profile in the coffin. He was numb, unable to accept that he would never see her again. Fingers laced in his lap, red eyes swollen, he stared at his shoes, only occasionally looking up. Each time he saw Jane's cheek, nose and peacefully closed eyes, he wondered why someone did not shake her until she woke up. Although he knew what death meant, it remained something that only happened to other people, people he did not know or had only heard about far, far away from his life.

The small white clapboard church stood like a beacon on the prairie with the steeple visible for several miles, no other structure around. There were few cars in the parking lot reflecting sparse attendance. Small groups of families and friends huddled together but plenty of open pews remained. Her life had been cut too short. Her circle of friends and acquaintances was small, but those in the community who had the great privilege of knowing her loved and admired her deeply, something not true of her family.

After about an hour, the preacher asked everyone to stand and led the congregation in a hymn followed by a prayer. The organist played a mournful religious melody. A smattering of soft weeping could be heard at various spots throughout the church, but no sound of mourning, whatsoever, came from the Ledbetter family.

The service ended. The Ledbetters left first by the side door. The remainder of the congregation filed by the open casket and then out the same side door. When Pop and the Bradshaw family emerged into the sunshine, Jane's family was waiting for the coffin to be loaded in the hearse.

Burton turned and pointed an accusing finger directly at Pop, then to Tom. "It's y'all's fault this happened."

The accusation took Marge's breath away. She placed her hand over her heart. "What are you saying, Mr. Ledbetter?"

"Your brat and your hired hand were meddlin' in our affairs. That's what the hell I'm sayin'."

Tom put his arm around Marge, but did not dignify Ledbetter's comment with a response. She had been stunned motionless and Tom had to pull her away.

"Go on Ledbetter," Pop said quietly, "Take care of the business at hand. Then, if you're capable, try noticing that you have two other children who need you. Hug 'em today...if you dare." Empathetic as it may have sounded, Pop's true feeling was much darker. Not lingering, he did not care if old man Ledbetter responded or not. He quickened his step, catching up to the Bradshaws, as they continued their solemn walk to the car.

The ride home was somber. They had known little Jane Ledbetter for only a short time but, now, each one of them mulled feelings of guilt and wondered aloud if there was anything they should have done to prevent the tragic loss, or if there was anything they needed to be doing for the family, especially the two surviving children.

Tom gave mumbling voice to thoughts of things left undone on the farm, but even the urgency of those matters could not hold his attention. He spoke for everyone in the car when he said, "It's sad to think the only time we really treasure the sanctity of life is when one is lost."

Colt heard it all but understood little of what they said. He just missed Jane. That's all he cared about.

It was late afternoon by the time Tom pulled the family sedan into the garage.

Pop went directly to his bedroom. He carefully removed his brand new khaki pants and shirt Marge had bought him for the funeral. He hung them with care in the closet.

Colt shuffled by his bedroom door, shoulders slung forward, head down. Pop called to him to come in. "Are you okay?" Pop asked, studying the youngster's face. "If you're feeling down, you can tell your ol' friend, Pop. You know that. Don't ya?"

The little man folded his arms to emulate his friend. "I'm worried about *you*."

Pop let his arms fall to his sides, totally taken aback with the comment. "Come over here and sit down for a minute," he said, pointing to the bed, as he pulled a ladderback chair in close for himself, slinging it around to sit on it backwards. His arms dangled over the top of the backrest.

Colt climbed up on the bed and sat on his hands in front of Pop. His little legs dangled, toes pointing inward.

"Why on earth would you be worrying about me?" Pop asked.

"Don't fill up the way Mr. Ledbetter did. Please?"

"What do you mean 'don't fill up'?" Pop asked, unconsciously stroking his freshly shaven face.

"You told me people could become empty of good things, and I thought you might be talking about yourself," Colt told him. "I just thought Mr. Ledbetter probably became empty, too, a long time ago. But he filled back up…with the bad stuff…you know, like hate. Please Pop, don't fill up like that…like Mr. Ledbetter did."

Pop smiled and patted the boy on the shoulder. "Not a chance. That's something you certainly don't need to worry about." After Colt jumped down and left Pop's room, the old man paced without purpose in the small bedroom and settled on standing in front of the window, looking out.

It had been a sunny spring day and the late afternoon shadows were long and dark, but Pop's attention was not on this natural beauty. The profundity of Colt's observation had so dazed the old man, he could not focus on anything else. Because it was true, he *had* been empty—so completely so, that the contemplation of suicide was a daily thing for a time.

Simply and in all innocence, Colt made him see that empty vessels can be filled again and that included the human emotional reservoir. He was in the process of filling his soul with a life-giving dose of love and hope, courtesy of Rodney Oliver Bradshaw, but he had not been conscious of it, until now. "Humph." *Fill up like Ledbetter? Not a chance little man, not a snowball's chance,* he thought.

A small, dirty bottle of pills and a still-sealed and heavily soiled bottle of cheap gin, his constant companions, his comfort zone for years, now, were nothing more than a disgusting piece of his history. Retrieving the sack from the drawer beside his bed, he dropped it into the wastebasket, no hesitation, no remorse.

He returned to his position at the window and noticed, this time, just how beautiful the long shadows of late afternoon were. Birds flitted about. A gentle breeze swayed the trees in time to a silent lullaby. The old man clasped his hands behind him and drew a deep, cleansing breath. Strangely, he could not remember the air smelling so sweet.

The lengthening shadows outside heralded the approach of a tranquil evening. The sight he witnessed was a world at peace. And that world, now, was his.

FOURTEEN

Spring rains set Bentley County ablaze with wildflowers, all sorts and all colors. The bluebonnets, mixed with the brilliant orange of Indian paintbrush, created a sight difficult, if not impossible, to duplicate on an artist's canvas. Native pasture along roadways flaunted beautiful colors on beds of lush green grasses.

The mood of the farming community reflected the scenery. The signs of a good start to the growing season abounded. Frequent moisture built substantial subsoil moisture to get crops started and rooted. Laughter and amiable chats were commonplace. The air filled with hope and faith that it would be a great year in farm country. It was a fickle thing. But, what might be described as a roller coaster industry was on the upside for the moment.

Only those chores absolutely necessary were tackled on Sundays at the Bradshaw's, but that was all. Feeding livestock, which had to be a seven-day-a-week task, and other minor emergencies that could not wait.

Colt enjoyed the calm, sunny afternoon tossing a ball high upon the roof of the barn and catching it in his often used and well-worn glove as it rolled off. He quickly tired of the solitude. He wanted someone to play with. He puffed air into his cheeks, threw down his ball and glove and walked with staunch determination to the house. He threw open the screened door, marched down the hall, and stopped abruptly at the living room. He surveyed the room as a general reviewing his troops. His eyes locked onto Pop. He sat in a corner chair, as was usually the case after chores were done. He quietly read a book. "Pop, I've decided you need some exercise."

The old man pulled his eyes away from the book reluctantly and saw the little man, arms folded, legs spread in that trademark pose. "Oh, you've decided that. Have you?" he said with an easy smile.

Tom entered the room, having heard the brash remark. "Now don't be disrespectful."

"The boy's probably making a pretty good diagnosis," Pop said, waving away Tom's concern.

Colt wrinkled his nose. "*Die egg*...what?"

Pop and Tom cut glances at one another and burst into laughter. "The word is *diagnosis*," Pop said. "It just means you probably figured right."

"Of course I figured right." He scampered down the hall to his room and returned with a bat. "Here, you can hit me some balls."

Pop saluted. "Okay Captain, lead the way." Marking his book, he followed Colt into the yard.

The entire family became involved in a lighthearted afternoon—the perfect American Sunday. Each taking a turn with the bat while the others fielded balls.

Pop pitched to Colt who swung and popped one over the old man's head. Pop stretched but missed and Colt took off running to an imaginary base as Marge picked up the ball and tossed it back to Pop who stepped sideways into Colt's path to tag him. Unable to stop, the little man bowled Pop over. Both tumbled to the ground laughing. Colt rolled over and groaned then smiled at the old man already back up on his feet.

"You know what? I'm tired. I think I'll quit now," Colt said, holding his side at the point his ribs made contact with Pop's knee. He rolled over to hands and knees and rose but was clearly fatigued.

Pop had a smile that simply would not go away, watching Colt head for the house and the pitcher of ice water in the refrigerator. But he did not return to the house right away, relishing the feeling brought on by the perfect afternoon. Tom and Marge eventually went back inside, too. Pop chose to sit on an upside down five-gallon bucket near the tool shed. He snapped a twig into pieces, flicking them toward a red ant mound, as he spent quiet time thinking. Over two hours passed. It was difficult to walk away from such a wonderful sensation that this day had offered up.

104

Gradually, other thoughts, not as pleasant, crept in. He knew that, soon, he would have to leave. Time grew short. He began the painful process of developing resolve. When the time came, he knew how difficult it would be—maybe the most difficult thing he would ever do. He refused to dwell upon a negative and went inside the house to join the family.

He noticed that Colt was unusually tired after his bath. The boy sat on the sofa staring blankly at television. He fell asleep before dark where he sat.

**

Over the next several days, Colt became increasingly lethargic. Marge thought it unusual that he had such a large bruise where he had run into Pop. It was not fading.

However, the lethargy was dismissed as spring fever. It probably would just take a few more days for the bruise to heal. In the week that followed, Marge received a call one afternoon from Colt's teacher who expressed concern because Colt's schoolwork had begun to suffer and observed he was becoming distant and inattentive. Having no school nurse in such a small country school, it was left to the teacher to report that Colt often nodded off in class and, on that day, suffered a minor bout of nausea. She suggested it might be related to a sinus or ear infection, or both.

Marge could no longer dismiss unusual behavior. The next day she kept Colt out of school to go to the doctor. He protested, not wanting to tarnish his otherwise perfect class attendance. The final day of the school year fast approached and summer vacation would be starting soon. He really looked forward to receiving that certificate for not having missed a single day all year. But, the appointment was set. His mother made it clear there would be no debating the issue.

Howard Tidwell, the Bradshaw's family physician, examined Colt. Young and aggressive, he had taken over when Doctor Brazzell retired the previous year. At first, Tom and Marge were apprehensive, since they had trusted Doctor Brazzell implicitly almost all their lives. But Doctor Tidwell had earned high marks from the Bradshaws for the care he had given Marge after her heart attack.

"Uh-huh," the doctor drawled, as he peered into every orifice in the boy's head and confirmed that Colt indeed had an infection of the sinus cavities and in both ears. He prescribed an antibiotic. "That should fix him up in about a week," he told Marge.

That afternoon Colt began the regimen and his medication seemed to have a quick effect. After a week, the nausea disappeared and, though feeling better, he continued pale and lethargic. The very next week Colt developed, what appeared to be, the flu. Once again, he was kept from school for yet another trip to the doctor.

This time, Doctor Tidwell was skeptical. It was not flu season. "I think we'd better take a blood sample and see if we might have something else at work here," he told Marge. "I'll call tomorrow afternoon. I should have the results back from the lab by then."

Although Marge and Tom were concerned, it was not overly so. They assumed it was something that could be fixed with medication, perhaps another antibiotic, once Doctor Tidwell specifically diagnosed it...maybe just a stronger antibiotic.

As for Pop, he had a different feeling, an unsettling sense of the situation. He sat with his little friend and talked at length about baseball, school and anything else that interested the little guy the night before the blood test results were expected. Colt fell asleep in mid-sentence, leaning against Pop on the sofa.

With a nod of approval from his parents, Pop picked up the lad and took him to bed, tucked him in and studied the boy's face. Colt's head sank into the fluffy pillow. The old man stood over him, thinking he seemed smaller than usual but shook it off, believing it probably stemmed from concern and created a misplaced sense that the boy was tiny and helpless. Pop gave the blanket a final tug to be sure Colt's shoulders were covered.

Noticing the brilliant full moon through the window, he paused to reflect. Having lost faith in deities many years ago, he still felt compelled to utter his own agnostic version of a prayer. "Mr. Moon," he said, looking through the window, face bathed in its soft glow, "this little guy needs your light more than ever now. I'm sure of it. Would you please shine on him?" He turned away, planning to end it there, but then looked back. "Please?"

The next day was steeped in cautious optimism. They waited for the call from the clinic. But, when it finally came, the receptionist refused to give any information over the phone. Instead, she asked them to meet Doctor Tidwell at his office within the hour for consultation. She said the doctor specifically requested they come without Colt.

"Damn it," Marge whispered, then looked up and apologized to God, "Sorry, Father." She dropped her earring for the second time, unable to get the hook through the pierced hole in the lobe. She walked to the kitchen, still fumbling with it. "Are you sure you don't mind watching Colt for a little while, Pop?"

"Oh, no ma'am," he replied without hesitation. "I'll fix something and see if I can get him interested in eating while you and Mr. Bradshaw are gone."

"Thanks, Pop," she said then turned to walk right into Tom who had come to join her. The nervous rush by them both was clear. They disappeared through the back door in a rush.

As Pop watched them leave, he became aware of a gnawing sensation in his gut.

His sense of things had not improved. Gloom settled then swelled like storm clouds on the horizon. He opened a can of brothy soup and heated it on the stove. All the while, he suspected it would be futile, but had to try and interest Colt in eating.

Pop took the steaming bowl to Colt who lay on the sofa, covered to the waist with a blanket. "Boy, you should eat something whether you feel hungry or not," he said.

"Why?" Colt struggled to support himself up on an elbow. "Why do I have to eat if I don't feel hungry?"

Pop sat down on the sofa beside him with the bowl in hand. "Well," he said, "food is to humans as gasoline is to a car. It's fuel. If we want to keep our engine runnin' we have to eat."

"Okay," Colt said and began to comply. Sitting up, he took the bowl from Pop and ate. With every spoonful, his little body sunk deeper into the sofa cushion for support. Eventually, he triumphed, eating the whole thing, handing the empty bowl to Pop then falling back over. It had taken great effort, but he struggled through it, because his best friend said it was the right thing to do.

"I'm sorry Pop," he said, "but my head hurts." Shortly afterwards, he vomited.

Pop stayed at his side and stroked his head with a wet cloth until he fell asleep. When Tom and Marge reappeared at the backdoor, Pop saw that both had red swollen eyes. That gnawing sensation was suddenly a knot. They had been crying. "Is it bad?" He did not want to be intrusive but was desperate to know.

Marge nodded and tried to speak, but choked and began crying again. She ran from the room.

Tom took off his Stetson and handled the hat like it was heavy and hung it on the rack near the backdoor. He leaned against the wall. "I'm afraid it couldn't be much worse," he said in a way that indicated a heavy heart weighed on each word. "Doctor Tidwell said he believes Colt has leukemia and fears it might be a fast-growing type called Acute Lymphocytic Leukemia. I don't really understand everything he told us, but the bottom line is we're taking him to M. D. Anderson in Houston for a bone marrow test, and if that's positive, we'll stay to begin chemotherapy immediately." Tom trudged by Pop on heavy legs. His shoulders slumped. He looked old and defeated.

Leaving was no longer an option for Pop. Plans had just changed.

FIFTEEN

The month of May began typically stormy. The seasons were again in the throes of change. Air masses battled for supremacy. Pacific fronts swept across northern Texas every three or four days. The area between the eastern plains of New Mexico on the west and the Caprock to the east seemed to catch the brunt of every weather system. This happened to be the location of Green Meadow. The cooler, drier air collided with warmer air south of it, forcing it high into the atmosphere. Towering thunderstorms resulted that became violent quickly. The turbulent, unpredictable weather turned out to be fortuitous for the Bradshaws. But, that only concerned the farming operation. Tom was in no frame of mind to notice such small, backhanded blessings.

Early in the season, before Colt's diagnosis, he had given thought to planting cotton and grain early. If he had, the young tender crops would have been subjected to two separate, but equally devastating, hailstorms. If the first had not wiped it out, the second one surely would have. As a consequence, the time he and Marge spent in Houston while Colt underwent chemotherapy did not cause him to miss anything on the farm, except wasting time and money on failed plantings. While at M. D. Anderson Hospital, he saved seed and fuel costs from a loss that could have been, but never was. That was the blessing Tom had difficulty giving thanks for. Too many other things crowded out that bit of good fortune. Colt was at the center of it all.

There was another side of the delicate balance over when to plant that Tom was painfully aware of; if cotton is not planted before the middle of June, in this part of Texas, the rule-of-thumb is that it will not be ready to harvest by first frost in the fall. Freezing temperatures might prematurely kill the plants and all would be lost. During Tom's farming career there had been several years he never planted cotton at all due to spring droughts. When rains finally did come, usually late in June, it was too late and he knew it. As contradictory as it may sound, weather is the farmers' best friend and his worst enemy, sometimes in the same season.

Now that the deadline fast approached to get that cottonseed in the ground, Tom had to act soon. The time to plot and plan was over, he could wait no longer. He left Marge and Colt in an apartment he rented temporarily in Houston and drove back to the farm. When he pulled up to the house, he sat for a moment, clutching the steering wheel with both hands and thought about how long he had been gone from home. He took a moment to reconsider how peaceful it was; something he too often took for granted. Only after an extended absence, as this was, did he notice such magnificence. The congestion and chaotic traffic of Houston emphasized it greatly. A renewed sense of hope washed over him, albeit fleeting. He stopped only twice during his eight-hour drive. He was exhausted.

Pop toted a bucket from the barn to the pen. Cows gathered, as they did every afternoon at feeding time. A clock could almost be set by their daily march to the pen. Chickens were underfoot, flapping and squawking. Their instinct equated a human holding a bucket to food. The bawling of the cows was interspersed with the occasional grunt or squeal from the hog pens. It was a symphony of good sounds, a mix of pungent aromas, things only a lifelong farmer could love.

Tom continued hanging on to the steering wheel with both hands, as if he might fall over without the support. He watched—just watched through the windshield for a while, feeling blessed and contented. *Pop showed up in our lives at the perfect time*, he thought. *More importantly, that he decided to stay.* He had had no idea angels came looking like a wiry little old man from the streets of Chicago. That thought was worth a crooked grin.

He watched Pop dump the supplement formula into a trough then monitor the activity for a few seconds to be sure the slick, shiny bovines had a chance at an equal share. There was no need for hay. The pastures were lush, the grazing better than in many previous years. Those early hailstorms were accompanied by soaking rains that propelled the grass upward into a tall carpet of green. A little supplement for vitamins and minerals was all that was needed to aid a rapid weight gain. Every quick pound of gain had a dollar sign attached to it and would be needed more this year than in most others.

Tom considered thinning his herd. Money moved to the forefront of most every thought these days. Selling off a few cows and hogs was an option—one he had to consider right now. There was no alternative. It had to be done. As this nagging thought weaseled in, it deepened his fatigue instantly. He got out of the car.

Pop had not noticed until the car door slammed. He hung the bucket on a fence post and started toward the house, shouting, "How's Colt? Any change?"

Tom rubbed his cheek with his broad weather-beaten hand. "Nah," he said, "The chemo seems to be doing about as much harm as good by my reckoning. Hell, I can't tell if it's the leukemia or that chemical soup they're stickin' in him that's makin' him so damned sick!"

Pop pursed his lips and nodded, but said nothing. All he could do was show concern. It ran deep. There was nothing he could say to make it seem better than it was.

"By all that's holy, Pop, if I weren't a Christian man, I'd..." Tom let it hang right there, rubbing his face briskly, like he was washing away disgust. "I'm sorry. Just a little tired that's all." Again, Pop nodded.

"Well, how are things here?" Tom asked, scanning the area.

"You've got two new calves."

"Thank God for that. We're going to need every marketable item we can lay our hands on by this fall, and, incidentally, we need to get the tractor and hitch it to the planter and service it. We have to get it field-ready right away. We only have about two weeks to get nearly four hundred acres of cotton seed in the ground."

"Mr. Bradshaw," Pop said, "Don't you think a good dinner and a night's rest would make you a little more efficient at the task?"

Tom just looked at the old man for a moment. "Yeah. Yeah, I guess it would." With all that was on his mind, rest had not been considered as part of the plan.

"You take a shower. I'll fix dinner." Pop spoke matter-of-factly and turned to go in to the house. An afterthought struck him. He slapped his forehead with the heel of his hand. "I meant to say supper. I'll become a Texan yet," he said then walked on.

"Yeah, supper," Tom whispered staring after him, realizing he needed Pop's grounding and objectivity, or he might do more harm than good in his haste. Instinct drove him, but his mind and heart was in Houston.

**

Over the next ten days, Tom made good progress, even with occasional downtime for repairs, adjustments, or to take care of business in Green Meadow. Pop continued his duties as housekeeper and livestock caretaker, but always eager to help out when more than two hands were called for.

Many times Tom caught himself sinking deeper into his thoughts, becoming consumed to the point of distraction, often losing sight of where he was, or what he was doing. The monotony of driving a slow-moving tractor to plant half-mile rows was not a mentally taxing chore. On most occasions, he could afford to let his mind drift, with no harm done. But, even if the odds of something going wrong are a hundred to one— that one time is bound to show up sooner or later.

On the northern boundary of the farm there had been an old fencerow at some point in the farm's history, which was no longer there except for a deeply buried and substantially large corner post. It had been left as a marker to separate the Bradshaw farm from the neighbor's property. Attached to the post was a deadman, an inexpensive device that consisted of heavy wire stretched diagonally from the top of a corner post to the ground and attached to rocks or other types of heavy weight buried well beneath the surface, making an extremely effective method of holding corner posts upright, providing tension on long runs of barbed wire.

One morning, Tom looked back over his left shoulder, keeping an eye on the equipment and, at the same time, watching birds swoop and pluck worms and bugs turned up by the plows. It was one of those times his mind was not strictly on business, contemplating other things and other places. All the while, he approached the post on the right.

Suddenly, the outside plow point caught the heavy wire of the deadman and jerked the tractor violently. From somewhere, a loud crack rang out. Tom knew instantly what had happened, but it was too late. The damage was done.

The heavy metal bar parallel to the ground holding all the planter mechanisms in place, the toolbar, was long and cumbersome. The leverage had snapped the bracket that held it to the tractor. The damage was major. Repairs would be costly, and time-consuming.

Money and time were two things the Bradshaw family had dwindling amounts of. It took the remainder of the afternoon to rig a temporary support with chains so the hydraulics could lift the toolbar high enough off the ground just to drive it back to the house.

Tired and dirty, Tom wasted no time in hurrying into the house and calling implement retailers in the area. It was a consensus among several dealers the bracket would have to be ordered from the manufacturer. Shipping would take a week, probably more. The only alternative was to buy a new planter, but that was not an option. Expense pushed it right out of the possible column.

In a flash, Tom was faced with two seemingly impossible choices; he could spend two hundred dollars, but lose a week or more of precious planting time, or spend eight thousand dollars and purchase a whole new unit and be planting again immediately. Dejected, he sat in the old ladderback wicker-bottomed chair, phone dangling loosely in his hand, and tried to think of a solution. But the only thing coming to him

113

was exhaustion—not answers. Dropping his hat to the floor between his feet, he hung up the phone as a final act of resignation.

Pop stood silent at a door behind Tom, peeking around at him, understanding fully the dilemma. "Mr. Bradshaw," he said, "Do you mind if I borrow the pickup truck for a little while? I need to, uh...I need to go in to Green Meadow to the store."

Without raising his head, Tom tossed him the keys and said, "Sure. Go ahead."

After Pop left, Tom remained motionless for a long time. The quiet was intense and crushing. As depression swarmed over him, he felt smaller and more inconsequential as the ring in his ears became louder. It may have been a defense mechanism, but his mind slipped into neutral, no more worrying, no more planning. He was just numb. The afternoon faded into evening. Only then did he rouse himself to shower and eat the meal Pop had prepared. Comfort provided by familiar rituals was miniscule, but he did what he normally did anyway. He trudged to his comfortable chair in front of the television. He pointed the remote and clicked it. But, it was a mindless gesture. Watching it did not interest him. Just a habit, it was the after-supper-thing-to-do.

He did not know how long Pop had been gone, or when he returned. He just knew that he woke in his chair when Pop gently nudged his shoulder. "Mr. Bradshaw," he said, "Why don't you go ahead and get in bed? I'll turn everything off in here." Tom staggered off to his bedroom.

Pop systematically walked through the house and turned off the lights and the television. Down the hall, Tom fell hard on the bed, springs creaking and groaning under his ample girth. "Sleep well Tom Bradshaw," he whispered, "Everything's going to be okay. I promise."

The next morning began very much the way the night before ended, with Tom in a confused state. He sat quietly eating breakfast. No new ideas came to him. But he knew he could not just sit and worry. That much he was certain of. He was a doer by nature and needed to be doing something—

anything. So, he announced he was going to weld the bracket together and see if it would hold long enough to finish planting.

All morning he wrestled with the heavy equipment to get it lined up and mated back the way it had been when it snapped. When he finally accomplished that, he grabbed his welding helmet, electrode holder and sat on his heels on top of the planter and began the tedious task of melting bead after bead of molten metal along the jagged break line in the thick steel bracket at all angles.

After lunch, feeling hopeful, he told Pop, "It's the moment of truth. I'm going to see if that weld is going to hold. I'm gonna take it down into the field and give it a test."

As Tom was about to leave the house, the phone rang. He stopped and watched Pop answer it. "Hello," he said then listened for a time. "Yeah, I think now would be a good time," he finally said. "Certainly. Come on."

"Anything I should be concerned with?" Tom asked.

"Nah. Not yet anyway."

Tom continued on out the backdoor with a renewed sense of vigor, jumped up onto the tractor and fired it up. The diesel engine belched black smoke and roared to life.

Tom had driven to the far side of the field and dropped the planter. He throttled up. The tractor roared. Then he backed it off. He glanced to the sky. "Please, Lord, make this work." He let out the clutch and the plows dug into the damp Texas soil. The smell of fresh turned earth and diesel mixed in the air, as the tractor groaned against the strain. He throttled up to regular planting speed.

About a hundred feet down the row, the tractor shuddered sideways following a loud pop. The weld failed.

Tom throttled the engine down and turned the key. The noise of the engine died away. All he heard then were gnats buzzing about his ears. There was no need to keep the tractor running. He was going nowhere. He sat backwards in his seat facing where he had come from and, once again, wrestled with the problem at hand. Unlike the night before, he was not despondent. Instead, the brutal truth lay before him and so were his options: There were none. Before he realized it, he was crying.

When he finally raised his head, he saw his pickup truck coming down the turnrow. Before he could wonder why, he noticed six tractors coming single-file, much farther behind it. He wiped the tears away, thinking that what he saw may have been a heat mirage, but a second look confirmed it. A caravan of tractors approached.

The pickup truck stopped abruptly in a brown cloud of dust and Pop hopped out.

"Pop, what the—"

"Before you say anything," the old man interrupted, "I need to tell you that I had a talk with your neighbor, Bud Landry, last night. I laid out what had happened and he said he'd take care of it. Now, I know you didn't give me permission to be saying anything about your problem, but I thought a desperate measure was needed to take care of a desperate situation."

He pointed to the approaching tractors; all outfitted with planters, and added, "I think you have some pretty darned nice neighbors who want to help." Dropping his head, smiling shyly, Pop stuffed his hands into his pockets and turned to watch the approaching tractors.

Tom was overcome with a sudden rush of emotion and frantically wiped the remaining tears from his eyes, not wanting his lifelong neighbors see him cry. Furthermore, he did not know what to say to Pop. "We may have to talk later about doing or saying things without permission, Pop," he blurted nervously, "But, for now, we have cotton to plant.

Pop's smile never wavered. "Yes, sir. I understand a reprimand might be necessary."

SIXTEEN

"Do you really think I look okay?" Colt rocked heel to toe and back, hands clasped in front, eager to know what Pop thought. The boy had grown gaunt, losing nearly twenty percent of his body weight; his skin tone had a greenish-gray cast, his eyes set in dark circles.

Pop studied Colt with a thoughtful smile. "Let's look at the facts, boy. It's the dog days of summer and your head'll stay cooler than most." Colt giggled, feeling his smooth pate. "Think about all those sports and movie stars who *prefer* having no hair at all. It's fashionable," Pop told him.

"*Fashin-bull.* What does *fashin-bull* mean?"

"It just means someone became tired of looking the same as everyone else and changed their look. When others noticed the change, they liked it and copied it. Once everyone was doing it, then it was fashionable." Pop ran his fingers through his own long, thin unruly hair. "Ya know what? I think it's about time I became fashionable, too." Slapping his knees, he sprang to his feet.

"I don't understand," Colt said.

"You just wait a minute." Pop fumbled through a nearby drawer in the kitchen, shoving the contents noisily this way and that, producing a pair of scissors. "Ah-hah! Found 'em." He grabbed a short stool and a cup towel on his way to the back door. "Well, come on. Follow me. I'll be needin' your help." Setting the stool in the shade of the large gnarled elm tree, Pop sat on it and tied the towel around his neck. "Okay Colt," he said, holding out the scissors, "Make me fashionable."

Colt giggled nervously. "What do you want me to do with those?"

"Cut my hair off," Pop said.

Colt's eyes grew large. "All of it?"

"Yep. All of it." He laughed then stopped abruptly and held Colt's scissor hand, adding with feigned seriousness, "You do know the difference between my hair and my ears...don't ya?"

Colt began cutting, his tongue firmly clenched between his teeth, concentrating on doing the best job possible.

The commotion caught the attention of Tom and Marge who worked in the garden, watering and picking tomatoes and black-eyed peas. The two moved furtively, trying not to draw attention and stay out of sight near the tool shed. They watched the old man and their young son share laughs, as hair fell in clumps to the ground with each snip.

The July heat could not melt the happiness in the air that afternoon, as only the occasional billowy cumulus cloud dotted the crystal blue sky. The most common outdoor activities, on these days, were swatting flying insects and mopping sweat with a handkerchief, but no one seemed to notice, or care, about such minor distractions.

Colt saw his momma and daddy watching. "I'm makin' Pop *fashin-bull*," he hollered. Tom and Marge joined them. Marge volunteered to finish the job with a razor. When the last of the stubble was shaved off, she handed Pop a mirror.

He looked at the handiwork. His deeply lined and tanned face stared back at him, in sharp contrast to the shiny white of a totally hairless scalp. He ran his hand over his head, amazed at its smoothness.

Colt took off his baseball cap and tossed it toward the porch. "We look just alike!" He stood next to Pop and both leaned forward, exposing two shiny, bald heads to Marge and Tom.

"Don't move," Marge said then chuckled. "Hold that pose." She ran into the house and retrieved a small camera and took all the remaining exposures on a partially used roll of film. She wanted to insure getting at least one, maybe two, really good pictures—pictures destined to become lifelong reminders of a blissfully happy moment.

Colt seemed to improve as the days passed. He tired easily and slept a lot, but the doctor said it was normal during the recovery process because his body had gone through so much from the disease and the treatment. Remission seemed possible.

Marge and Tom spent every available minute doting on him. Colt did not see that as strange. As far as he was concerned, that was the way it should have been all along.

It was not necessary for Pop to try and spend time with the boy, since Colt shadowed him and followed him everywhere, usually chattering on about anything and everything on his mind.

Late summer heightened fears of a money shortage. Although insurance helped with Colt's treatment, the incidental expenses were tremendous and ongoing. On occasion, Pop overheard Tom and Marge discuss selling off equipment or land parcels. It was an idea that had gone beyond possible and now approached probable.

It was a Saturday afternoon in early August. Marge had just written Pop's weekly paycheck. She laid it on the worn and well-used three-legged corner table in his bedroom, which had become the accepted way. She thought no more of it.

Getting dressed up a little and going into Green Meadow on a Saturday afternoon was a ritual in farm country. The adults shopped or just sat on benches around the courthouse square to recuperate and recharge from the hard week just finished, preparing for the one ahead. Colt approached his mother. "Are we going to town?"

Marge, at her sewing machine, patched worn clothing to extend their life a few more months. "Not today, Hon," she said, "I don't think we can spare the time."

"Aw, why not?" Colt whined.

"Well," she said with a sigh, "we just have too many things that need doing here at home, that's all." She never took her eyes away from the denim scrap she stitched onto a faded pair of blue jeans.

"But you promised we could and I—"

119

"Colt!" she exploded. "I don't have time!" The harsh words were out before she could stop. As Colt ran from the room crying, he brushed by Pop in the hall.

It was an attack born of frustration. She knew it was absurd and wilted forward until her forehead touched the sewing machine. "Damn," she muttered. "What am I doing? What in hell am I doing?" She began to cry softly. Several minutes passed then she heard soft footfalls behind her and quickly wiped away tears with embarrassed swipes.

"Mrs. Bradshaw?" Raising her head, she looked over her shoulder into Pop's sympathetic eyes. "I know it's none of my business, but maybe this is what you need to find the time to take Colt to town." He stuck two fingers in his shirt pocket and retrieved his folded paycheck. He dropped it in front of her.

"Oh, no," she protested, "You've earned that. It's yours."

"Yes ma'am. I agree wholeheartedly. It is mine. That means I should be free to do anything I please with it. And, it would please me greatly if you and Mr. Bradshaw would take Colt to town and just enjoy the afternoon." And with that, he left the room before her shock dissipated and had time to think of another reason why she could not take the money.

Over the Bradshaws' objections, Pop accepted no more payments for his work. The few checks they insisted on writing, he refused to cash. He began to see his time at the Bradshaw farm as a blessed life-altering experience, for which he did not deserve payment. His acceptance and presence were payment enough. If anything, *he* should pay. His stay was transforming into a life's mission, a mission that dictated he lift as many burdens from this family as was in his power. Having a purpose had eluded him for so many years it felt strangely exhilarating. He embraced it, the mission and the purpose.

He suddenly remembered the cloud game he had played with Colt in the field and his interpretation of what Colt saw in them. The explanation he gave Colt was becoming more personal than he ever imagined, a long road that ended at people in need of lifting up. *The wisdom of a child; am I the only one that knows the prodigy he is?*

120

SEVENTEEN

The summer grew long and unbearably hot at times. The doldrums became common after several weeks of unabated heat, but circumstances made it seem more oppressive and confining than usual. Tempers quickly surfaced. Extra effort became necessary to maintain civility.

Even in his young, inexperienced mind, Colt knew it wasn't normal, noticing the frequency of arguments between his parents. He just did not understand why. His hair grew back. He had been feeling pretty good and just wanted to play, unaware his disease lay like a stalking beast of prey waiting for its time. The last white cell count had risen.

Colt put all thoughts and energies into starting second grade. To him, there was nothing more important than that. His sickness had been diagnosed in the spring, before school let out for summer. School officials agreed his work was satisfactory enough to allow him to advance, despite time missed at the end of the school year. In the first grade there was little work that could be made up anyway.

Tom worried about the outcome of the current crop more than any year he remembered, since he foresaw the probability of Colt enduring another lengthy bout of chemotherapy and all the expenses that went along with it.

It was late August. Rains ended in early June. There had been no more. Though it seemed dire, it was common for a dry summer to follow a stormy spring. Nonetheless, Tom worried, not for more rain but for no rain at all. It was too late in the season. Rain would have done more harm than good in the late stages of cotton development, because it triggers the growth cycle. Plants would drop blooms and, more importantly, small bolls that still had a shot at maturity before frost. Rain would have transferred energy into growing the stalk, which is not good late in the cycle of maturation before harvest. Even mature bolls might not develop properly if the

121

plant ceased maturing and began a growth spurt, locking them shut at frost, turning them into black hard knots with absolutely no value.

Every afternoon that a cloud lifted and towered skyward, Tom stood by a window or the door, watching until the threat passed, sometimes an hour or more. But, it was more than simple observation; it was an agonizing, almost paralyzing fear. It consumed him.

There were so many things that could go wrong, Tom had fallen into the habit of sneaking down to the barn where he had hidden bottles of liquor in the little office, tucked in the corner behind feed sacks. It was the same room Pop stayed in when he first arrived. Tom locked the door behind him; threw his hat onto the worn desk and collapsed with a bottle onto the old, threadbare sofa. This escape worked well in the beginning. But, it took more and more to dull the torment of uncertainty—uncertainty of farming and, most important of all, not knowing what the future held for his only child. No one can know the future, but Tom felt more was out of his control than people should have to deal with. He did not realize the control he still possessed slipped away with each visit to the little office in the barn and with each swig from the bottle.

Marge was aware of the problem. It was a part of every argument, but to them it was a private family matter that concerned no one else. They asked for no help, and expected none. Like most Texas farm families, they were a highly self-sufficient breed of people who were always more than willing to offer help but rarely sought it, even from close friends and neighbors, although help was always offered and given automatically. It was a tight knit, almost closed society, very difficult for an outsider to understand or appreciate. Pop learned this and did not wait to be asked for help. It was simply his duty as a friend.

Pop stood back, observing. He contributed wherever he could. Marge did more and more of the work in the house because she needed to be busy. The old man watched Tom and took note of every trip he made to the barn and knew from first-hand experience where those little trips would end up and knew he must eventually intervene. Colt provided the correct timing for such an intervention.

One evening after supper Tom announced he was going to check on the cows and maybe work on his books for a while in the little office in the barn. It was a transparent excuse. No one questioned it. If Tom knew they were aware of what he did, he did not care. He had been down there for over an hour.

Colt decided it was time to see what kept his daddy so busy lately. He marched out of the house down by the machine shed and kicked at a chicken in his path. It squawked and flew off low in a cloud of dust and flying feathers. Undaunted, the young man pressed on with his self-assigned mission into the barn and up to the office door. He reached for the knob but stopped short. He heard the sound of mumbling and what seemed like someone softly weeping. He did not know what to think of that. Instinctively, he decided not to disturb his daddy. But, that only heightened his curiosity. Backing away, he walked around the outside of the barn to the single window and tiptoed in the knee-high grass to peak over the sill to see his father lying on his back on the sofa, his left arm draped over his eyes and a partially emptied bottle on the floor with his other hand wrapped around the neck of it.

Understanding only that his father was unhappy, the little man dropped down and stood, as he always did when he became determined, legs spread wide and arms folded over a proud chest. He puffed air into his cheeks, blew it out, pursed his lips and muttered, "Yep, that's what I need to do."

Marching back up to the house, he threw open the door, walked lively down the hall around the corner into the kitchen and, without delay, announced, "Momma, we need a party."

"A party?" Marge said without interest or expression, thinking this might be one of those times to simply humor the lad.

"Yeah. We can call it a back-to-school party or, hey, maybe an end-of-summer party." He became excited at the prospect of it. Pop heard the excitement in his voice and joined them in the kitchen, casually leaning against the wall separating it from the back hall.

123

"Colt," Marge said, "I'm afraid it would be just too expensive and—"

"Momma," he said then paused a single second. He added slowly and distinctly, "Daddy...needs...a party." The authority in his voice shocked her to silence. The depth and inflection of it easily disguised his age.

She stood with her mouth open, not believing what he had said and, more importantly, *how* he said it, wondering if a reprimand was called for or, maybe, a compliment for such intuitive boldness. "Well, Colt, you know there's a lot of planning involved, things to prepare..." She tapped her lip with a fingertip searching for words.

Taking the cue from the brief silence, "Ma'am, if you don't mind me saying so," Pop told her, "I don't think it's necessary to invest much money or time in such a get-together. It can be a potluck affair with everyone invited to bring a dish. We could provide drinks and, possibly, make ice cream. We could set up the horse shoe stakes and maybe that volleyball net I saw in the barn."

"Yeah, Momma! Yeah!" Colt jumped up and down.

She smoothed his hair which had grown almost enough to lay. "Okay guys, you win," she said. "But let it be known right now," she added, wagging her finger at them both, "You've opened yourselves up for some work."

Pop gave Colt thumbs up and a high-five slap. They sauntered away together, Pop's arm around Colt's neck and the youngster's arm around the old man's waist. There suddenly was cause for smiles around the Bradshaw house that afternoon.

Later that evening, after Colt had fallen asleep, Pop slipped out of the house and down to the barn. The old man figured it was time to get involved. His plan was to lay it on the line with his employer, his friend, and the father of his *best* friend.

He knocked on the door. No answer. He knocked again. He heard Tom mumble, "Go away."

"I don't think so boss," he mumbled right back, not caring if he was heard or not. He put his shoulder into the door and forced it open. The jamb was so loose it provided little resistance.

"I thought I said go away," Tom slobbered and slurred. His eyes searched the vicinity of the noise, trying to focus on the intruder.

Pop ignored it. "Mr. Bradshaw I'm going to say something and I don't need or want you to respond. But I do want you to *hear and comprehend* it. Can you sober up long enough to do that?"

Tom looked at him through the eyes of a drunk. His head drifted side to side. His lower jaw hung loose.

"Mr. Bradshaw, can you understand me?"

Tom nodded.

Pop paced in a tight circle as a warrior might before a big battle. The little old man was no longer a homeless whipped pup, but a self-declared mentor determined to keep a family together. With each step he grew straighter, his resolve deepened.

A hint of sobriety crept in, as Tom watched the scene unfolding in front of him. It was an awkward struggle, but after a couple of failed attempts, he sat up.

The old man suddenly stopped pacing. His hands locked behind him, he spun around to face Tom. "Mr. Bradshaw," he said, "I want to tell you a story that is pertinent to your situation. I'll skip many details but rest assured, it's quite true." Slinging a rickety old desk chair around to face the sofa, Pop sat down. "There was once a man who began life in a wealthy family and lived an upbringing of privilege. As advantage offered, this fellow graduated from one of the finest universities east of the Mississippi and went on to be a respected vice president of a nationally recognized brokerage firm. He married a lovely woman and had two beautiful daughters who were given anything they wanted. This guy had everything. He always had everything and couldn't imagine living life any other way." Pop stopped to collect his thoughts.

"Sounds like a great story," Tom said, "but the guy you're talking about is certainly nothing like me." His swimming eyes still struggled to focus.

125

Pop held up a hand. "Please, hear me out." He stood and again paced in front of Tom. "A day came that his wife decided her way of life was not good enough. Our prosperous businessman came home one day to discover a note, with no details, saying simply she was leaving and taking their daughters with her."

He almost choked on those words. A pained expression pulled down his brow. He paused and swallowed hard. "The reason, or reasons, for that decision will never be known or understood. This type of pain and uncertainty were totally foreign to him."

To seize the moment, Pop shoved a chair in close to Tom and sat facing him, only inches from his face. "But the story doesn't end there," he said. "Before the woman and two precious girls could even get out of town, a carload of celebrating teenagers ran a red traffic light at high speed crashing into their car, killing all three of them. Within the span of a few hours, this man experienced the pains of rejection, failure and, then, tremendous loss. Any one of the three would have been devastating, but all three simultaneously was a one-way ticket to hell."

Tom shifted on the old sofa; clearly uncomfortable at the direction Pop's story was taking. He looked more sober by the second. "The weeks that followed were a blur," Pop said, "But he tried desperately to get on with his life. He discovered the only way he could function was to dull the pain with liquor and whatever pills he could lay his hands on." He gazed deeply into Tom's eyes and added, "Can you see where this story is going now?"

Tom sat up straight, rubbing the stiffness from his shoulders. His face flushed with embarrassment. "Each day that passed," Pop said, "it took more and more liquor to get him through the day, until it finally cost him a multi-million dollar deal that his firm had put full faith in him to secure." He changed his tone and inflection, speaking low and slow for emphasis. "It had become impossible for him to render competent decisions. This man lost his position, his home, his family, and the respect of his friends. Hell, he lost everything!"

Shaken by the disturbing power of the words coming from his own mouth, Pop stopped talking abruptly and looked down before he lost control of his emotions. "A stinking liquor bottle became his best friend," he said with a voice filled with disgust. He drew a deep breath. "One day he woke up, sprawled on a dirty, littered floor without a single notion where he was. He was nasty. He stunk of alcohol. He was lost. Realizing only one thing, and that was just how deep the pit of humanity can be, as he watched a rat walk across his leg, as if the rodent believed him a fixture in that place. This guy not only saw the bottom...he was there."

Pop was drained. He was sure he looked it, too. Standing, still facing Tom, he said in a strong, calm voice, "You, my friend, are not there yet. But you're heading toward it. And, it would seem, you're hell-bent on getting there. You have to stop what you're doing. You have to take control before it's too late." He turned and shoved his chair back toward the desk and took a couple of steps toward the door.

"Did he make it?"

Pop stopped and looked back at Tom over his shoulder.

"The man in the story, did he make it?" Tom repeated.

The old man turned and slowly raised his eyes to meet Tom's. "I can't answer that question...yet. But I *can* say, that that day, lying on the floor in that abandoned building, was the day Paul Odell Peterson died and Pop was born.

EIGHTEEN

A full year would soon be coming to an end since Pop had moved in with the Bradshaws. September was just around the corner. He noticed weeds, some large enough to dwarf waist-high cotton, scattered across the field. This year, he did not need to be compensated, or even persuaded. He sharpened a hoe and went to work taking the matter into his own hands. The few small weeds the hoe hands missed earlier in the month were now large and potentially devastating to the machinery of the cotton picker. It was not only damaging to the equipment but could easily create costly delays when time would be premium. This was a crop year in which everything had to go perfectly. There was so much at stake. Failure was not an option. The weed problem would only take a few days and not as great a problem as it was the year before.

Pop had another, more immediate reason for staying busy outside the house. He needed to stay away, so Marge and Tom could work out their burgeoning problems in private. He knew they would say nothing in his presence if he failed to take the initiative to stay away. They were just that polite. But they needed the opportunity to unlock those carefully guarded problems and turn them loose to walk through the fire of discontent, the darkness, and then, hopefully, into the brighter light of solutions. Pop knew they needed their privacy and given the latitude to talk as they pleased. Otherwise, it might fester into more serious marital problems. Although it may have been what they needed, Pop cringed when he heard shouting coming from inside the house and he was still some distance away.

Wanting his companionship, Pop yearned to ask Colt to help him, but he resisted doing so. He believed the little guy might be too weak for such strenuous activity. So the first two days seemed to grind slowly. It was tedious without the

129

youngster to keep him from miring in his thoughts. He missed the little man's chatter and companionship.

On the third morning, Pop picked up his hoe, tightened it in a vice outside the machine shed and honed the edge with a file. As he did, he heard a commotion and looked up to see Colt bounding out of the house. Shouting from a distance, "Hey Pop! Ya want some company today?"

The shrillness of his voice evoked a cacophony across the yard. Calves bawled, pigs squealed and chickens cackled. It was conditioning, if a human voice was near, something to eat was sure to follow. "That'd be fine," he hollered back blandly, not wanting to betray his joy.

"I'll help pull those big ol' weeds out of the cotton rows for ya."

Pop lifted the freshly sharpened hoe and blew the metal shavings from it. He sighted down the honed edge with one eye, inspecting his work with the file. "Do only what you feel like doing. Don't overexert yourself," he said, looking down at his little friend. Raising an eyebrow, he added, "Deal?"

"*Over ezert.* What does that mean?"

Pop rested the hoe on his shoulder and held it with one hand while taking the boy's hand in the other. "Just take it easy. That's all it means." With that, they headed for the cotton patch.

The first couple of hours went quickly. Pop cut weeds and Colt pulled them, one by one, out of the rows. The boy was his usual chatty self for a time, and the old man patiently listened, answering Colt's questions with as few words as possible.

Pop worked on down the row, suddenly noticing Colt had gone quiet. Looking back, he saw Colt lagged behind about fifty feet, standing slumped over with his hands on his knees, his breathing labored. Pop dropped his hoe and hurried back to him. "Are you okay, boy?"

Still slumped over, Colt looked up, one eye closed, squinting with the other, blinded by the sun beyond Pop. "Is it okay to rest a minute?" he asked then shaded his eyes.

Pop dropped into the shade of the waist-high cotton stalks and fell back on his elbows. "Does this answer your question?"

Colt lay with his head on Pop's leg. After a time, his breathing eased. They did not talk for the first few minutes, just enjoying the shade and the breeze. The only sounds were the distant drone of a single-engine airplane and the occasional buzzing insect.

"Pop?"

"Yeah."

"I know I said Daddy needed a party but, ya know what? I think Momma needs one just as bad." He raised himself up and looked at the old man. "Don't you?"

Pop nodded. "I think 'party' is as good a word as any to explain what they need." Pop admired Colt's innate wisdom. Although not understanding the change in his parents, he certainly saw and felt it. The old man guessed the boy was willing to take on the burden of his parent's happiness.

Colt sat bolt upright and twisted around to face the old man. "Pop," he said in a rush, "When I grow up, I want you and me to be partners."

The old man sat up, too, and brushed the dirt from his elbows. "Partners, huh? Doin' what?"

"Oh, heck. It doesn't matter. I think that together, we can do just about anything."

Pop swallowed. But a sudden lump in his throat hung fast. He coughed to clear it away. "Maybe so. But right now, I think you need to go back to the house and lie down. It's time for you to rest."

Colt jumped up and said, "Okay, but we should talk more about this. Right, partner?" He stuck his hand out to Pop.

"Right...partner," Pop said then took Colt's hand and shook it.

The boy marched away in time to that music only he could hear. But the march, the little guy's trademark, was interrupted by a stumble. He could not notice the difference in himself, but Pop saw the weakness growing in his frail little body.

Colt said over his shoulder, "Don't stay out here too long. Saturday is only two days away and we have a party to get ready for." After a few more steps, he added, "Oh, yeah, be sure and shave before Saturday, too."

Pop worked without Colt the remainder of the day. His only company was that tenacious lump in his throat.

**

On Saturday, a steady stream of cars drove up the long tree-lined lane to the Bradshaw home. The handwritten fliers posted at the small country church down the road and the grocery store in Green Meadow worked far better than they could have imagined. Word-of-mouth took over where the paper notices left off and, judging by the number of cars, many families in this north Texas community were just as ready as the Bradshaws for a diversion from the doldrums of summer.

Marge rung her hands with worry, thinking there would not be enough food or drink. But, her concern proved unfounded, since all the arriving guests produced casseroles, sandwiches, chips and melons. The variety of food and drink was astonishing.

Handshakes and hugs were shared as people made their way into the backyard and enjoyed the time-accepted tradition of gossip and talk. Weather and crops was the icebreaker for every conversation. The Arnold family brought a boom-box and plugged it into the extension cord by the elm tree. Country music blared, creating the perfect atmosphere for such a gathering.

Colt and Pop had done a great job with preparations. Pop had hung lights in the big elm tree in the backyard and Colt helped him set a sheet of plywood over two sawhorses to create a temporary table for the food. All too soon, it proved inadequate to handle the amount of goodies covering its surface. Another was needed just to hold all the casseroles and other great things from neighboring kitchens. The sound of laughter and children playing filled the air, underscoring the steady grumble and grind of the ice cream machine.

During the afternoon, Pop was cordial to everyone, but preferred staying in the background. It was enjoyable just as it was. The day was hot but otherwise, perfect. No one seemed to mind the heat. Every place a tree or building cast a shadow, people claimed squatter's rights to the cooler shade. Plenty of cold drinks and watermelons bobbed in ice water in a small trough. He leaned against the elm tree and surveyed the goings-on.

A group of men took over the horseshoe pit situated in the shadow of the barn and were locked in friendly competition, joking loudly with one another on their unpracticed skills with the shoes. Some of the older kids played volleyball and small groups of people, scattered about, just visited and enjoyed the day.

At one point, Pop felt the wind change. He turned his nose into the northerly breeze and the temperature seemed to dip just a degree or two. He held his face up and closed his eyes for a moment. It was probably a weak cool front that no one else noticed. But, it reminded him that the seasons would soon be changing. There was sadness in that thought. Even the heat could not keep a shiver from coursing his spine.

Tom's oldest friend, Bobby Joe Peeler and his family arrived and the two men peeled away from a group of farmers to sit on a large, partially rotted cable spool in the shade of the little machine shed just off the backyard, laughing and trading jokes.

Pop watched them, Tom in particular, for the longest time, studying his behavior, as a doctor would a patient to determine a prognosis. Thinking Tom may have turned the corner, he was hopeful he had gotten through to him. He did not care to dwell on such a thing on a day like this but it raced through his mind that Tom would need every ounce of emotional strength he could muster over the next few weeks and months. He turned away and looked elsewhere, trying to bring his mood back to a happier place.

"Come on Pop. Play with us." Colt shouted gleefully, running by with two of his school buddies. But the boy had no intention of waiting for an answer, far too busy having a good

133

time. He disappeared around the corner toward the front of the house.

Marge seemed content to busy herself with playing the role of hostess, making sure food and drinks were readily available. She chatted with anyone willing to stand still for a time.

As the day passed and shadows lengthened, the noise of the crowd became more subdued, but no less friendly. The widow, Ella Minyard, latched on to Pop's forearm, holding tight. She chatted about anything crossing her mind. It was obvious she did not want to let him go and traded one subject for another, trying to get him interested in talking. If she wanted answers to her questions, she was not pausing long enough for him to formulate answers. He assumed she did not. Therefore, he did not even attempt to answer. The smile on his face was fixed and insincere. He did not want to be rude, but he did want her to go away. He was cornered, no options for a quick escape. But he pleasantly protested by not making eye contact. Her infatuation was of no concern to him. His absolute lack of interest may have come through—finally. She eventually tired of the game and moved on. With a long sigh of relief, Pop returned his attention—his full attention—to the party, realizing that it had been some time since he had last seen Colt. He moved away from the elm tree for the first time in over an hour and began looking for the boy.

Marge shooed flies away from the array food on the makeshift tables. Tom and Bobby Joe still went at it over by the machine shed. After making a round, Pop became even more anxious when the two boys he had been playing with came running toward him without Colt. He snared one by the arm as he ran by. "Hey, have you guys seen Colt?"

"Uh-uh," said one.

"No, sir," said the other. "Not for a while."

Pop stood, hands on hips, looking first this way then that. There were many places the boy could be, since the area beyond the backyard was cluttered with outbuildings and large farm implements everywhere. The sights and sounds of the party slipped into the background. He only wanted to see and hear one person. Colt. And, he did not. He made a special effort not to alarm anyone. He did not call out the little guy's name, but searched from one place to the next. With each empty hiding place, his pace quickened. Walking around the house to the front yard, where no guests had gone, he examined a small ornamental windmill, standing about six feet tall with jasmine threading through it in a tight jumble. The fan blades turned slowly, responding to the tiniest shifts in the wind, squeaking on each full revolution. "Colt are you there?" Pop called out in a low voice.

The reply was weak, but unmistakable. "Over here." On the other side of the windmill, he found Colt lying on his side, his knees drawn up to his chin. He had vomited.

The old man fell to his knees. "My God, boy…"

The little man did not move. "Please, don't tell Momma and Daddy," he whispered. "They're havin' so much fun…feelin' so good right now."

"I-I can't make you that promise, Colt," Pop told him. "You're sick."

"Please Pop." Colt struggled to look into the old man's eyes. "You gotta promise. You just gotta. It's all I…it's all…it's all I ever…" His weak voiced trailed off.

Anguished, Pop glanced skyward then scooped Colt up into his arms. The little man slipped from consciousness. Tears were all that Pop had left.

NINETEEN

Colt's future and fate were sealed, reduced to a simple matter of when, though why would still be asked. He lay in a bed on the third floor of the Bentley County Hospital in Green Meadow, drifting in and out of consciousness, too weak for more chemotherapy. His condition worsened, leaving the Bradshaws and Pop—even Doctor Tidwell, sad and confused. All options had run out. Every tick of the clock matched aching hearts, as Colt Bradshaw's life siphoned away.

Pop finished the morning feeding chores and drove the old pickup truck into town to visit his little friend. It was difficult to imagine; only four days had passed since Colt had been running and laughing. The sound of that laughter repeated in an endless, reverberating loop in the old man's mind. Now, as Colt's life leached away, his lucidity diminished by the hour. Gingerly opening the door to Colt's room, Pop entered and found Marge sitting on the edge of the bed holding the youngster's hand. She and Tom bore the faces of sorrow.

"Any change?" he said softly, gliding around the bed. Their expressions were the only answer he needed. Pop patted the boy's arm. "Hang in there little man," he said in a breathy whisper.

Colt's eyes fluttered and opened, searching for his friend—his best friend. He tried to focus. But swimming eyes indicated whatever he saw was not clearly defined. He smiled. "Hey Pop. Still partners. Right?"

"Partners. Always."

"Jane was here last night." His voice faltered. "She came just to see me. How about that?"

"Jane?"

"Yeah. She sat with me for a long time and talked about…" He swallowed with difficulty, "about how wonderful things were where she moved to and how good and happy she felt. Pop, she told me we'd be together real soon." Those words took a measure of strength he could ill afford and closed his eyes, quiet for a time, then, "I wish you could have been here. My two best friends, right here with me...same place...same time..." his voice trailed away. He appeared to lose consciousness.

Pop could not handle it any longer. Emotion swarmed him. He turned to Marge and Tom, pursed his lips tight, backed away and left the room. He fought the powerful urge to curse God for allowing it to happen; yet, he remained composed until the elevator doors closed behind him. Then, he could hold it no longer. The same crushing feeling of loss, he last felt twenty-two years ago, overwhelmed him. He gasped for air and banged his fists on the elevator walls. A montage of images gorged Pop. He began a downward spiral into despair. He felt as though he were suffocating.

Walking aimlessly, he emerged from the alley beside the health care facility then on across the street, down the block and into an alley between the Co-op Feed Store and a vacant lot. Turning the corner, he found himself behind Max's High Plains Feed Store.

An old pickup truck was backed up and parked against the loading dock. Burton Ledbetter tossed the last of several fifty pound bags from the dock into the bed of the truck. He mopped sweat from his bald head with a dirty rag he produced from the hip pocket of faded blue bib overalls. He noticed Pop. "Hey you," he yelled out then squatted on his haunches and looked down at Pop with an accusing finger stretched in the old man's direction. "I hope you remember, we still have unfinished business to tend to." He grinned the Ledbetter grin. "You Yankee piece o' shit." He sat for a few seconds, clearly hoping for a burst of anger from the old man. He then dropped off the edge of the loading dock.

Pop kept walking. He made no indication he heard or even had seen Ledbetter. He kept his head down and his hands stuffed deep into his pockets. His mind was on more important things and did not care about a sub-human with an attitude. He walked on with every intention of not acknowledging any of it.

The old man's disinterested silence was Ledbetter's cue to ratchet it up. "Hey!" He yelled sharply. "I heard the Bradshaw brat was in bad shape in the hospital. Is that right? Those little shits are more trouble than they're worth sometimes. Aren't they?"

Nothing was going to stop Pop from moving on, until that. He froze. Turning slowly, he pulled his hands from his pockets and began walking back in Ledbetter's direction. The closer Pop came, the angrier he became, walking faster and faster then trotting. As his speed increased, his mood went from sadness to annoyance to blind rage in the blink of any eye. He clenched his fists and, from the primal depths of his gut, he screamed. Bridled anger that had been bottled for twenty-two years was about to be unleashed.

"Bring it on you little sonofabitch," Ledbetter snarled.

Pop moved like a man half his age driving himself into the stinking farmer with such force that the sweaty hulk stumbled backwards into the loading platform, but Pop's advantage was quickly lost.

Ledbetter hurled a giant fist into Pop's temple with solid impact, sending him dazed and reeling. Pop slammed against the side of the pickup truck. His knees buckled. He slid down the truck, landing on his butt hard. It knocked the wind from him.

Eyes fluttering, he tried to quickly clear his vision, but did not need to analyze the situation to know one more punch like that and he would be out cold. Without taking his eyes away from the blurry image of the approaching behemoth, his hands swept the powdery dust on the ground at his sides as he searched desperately among the litter and debris scattered about for anything he could use as a weapon.

Ledbetter stalked, like a lion going for the kill, confidently, with no fear of failure. Clamping Pop's head between his huge hands, as though he was about to crush a melon, he slammed the old man's head against the truck.

Pop saw a bright flash and, for a split-second, the world went black, as his searching hand found something solid in the dirt and slung it upward defensively. A gagging sound was followed by the dull thump of a body hitting the ground.

It took several seconds for Pop's vision to clear. When it did, there lay Ledbetter on his back with a triangular piece of jagged metal embedded in his throat.

Pop sat motionless and stunned. He had trouble comprehending that he had done that. He then fell over on his hands and knees and hurriedly crawled to his adversary, still unable to stand.

Ledbetter's eyes were wide open, as if searching the sky for answers and his mouth just as wide, trying to draw air. Pop yanked the blood-smeared shard from Ledbetter's throat; hoping life-giving air could then pass through. It was too late.

Suddenly, Ledbetter's body fell limp. Even one more breath was not forthcoming. His heart stopped and the pumping blood did, too, although it continued flowing from the gash. His eyes glazed into a lifeless stare. His hands still clutched at his throat. Blood dripped from those fingertips.

Max Garza, the owner of the feed store, heard the commotion and came out onto the loading dock and saw Pop kneeling over Ledbetter holding that metal scrap. "What the hell have you done?" he yelled, turning to run back into the store.

Pop knew Max would call the sheriff. He also knew how it appeared. He had no witnesses. He was a relative stranger in town. There was no doubt in his mind what would happen if he waited for a sheriff's deputy to arrive. He ran, stumbling, dazed from the blows to the head. He had to find some place safe, while he thought all this through.

Pop zigzagged through alleys, backyards and side streets, searching for a place he could hide. Stopping frequently to lean against trees, buildings, signs, or just about anything, but only for a second or two each time. His head pounded with pain and confusion. He had to keep moving and get as far away from that feed store as possible.

A dilapidated vacant house, virtually hidden by an overgrowth of trees and bushes came into view on an unpaved side street. Running through the open door that hung by only one remaining hinge and over piles of crumbling sheetrock, he quickly decided it would not be safe enough and moved on through it into the backyard. He noticed a piece of warped and weather-worn plywood laying slightly askew atop a hole in the ground. He lifted it and saw that it covered the stairs of an old cellar and quickly stepped down into it, sliding the plywood back over the entrance. With luck, if they searched the yard, it would appear to simply be another discarded piece of junk, among the many strewn about.

He sat in the cool, musty darkness on the powdery dust covering the floor. His breathing had not yet settled. Dirt laced sweat stung his eyes. His mind raced with possible ways he might get away without detection.

Sirens wailed in the distance. The search for him had begun. Finally, after his breathing returned to a deep, even pattern, he began to think more clearly. Although he did not consider himself inhumane or cruel, Pop felt absolutely no remorse for what he had done. If anything, he had sacrificed himself to rid a wonderful community of a cancer—a cancer by the name of Ledbetter. *Besides, it was an act of self-defense. If I hadn't stopped Ledbetter, it would've been me lying dead in the dirt and Ledbetter would have gone free to continue spewing his venom.*

His eyes searched the cramped darkness for answers and fixed upon a tiny ray of light penetrating a nail hole in the plywood above him. The beam struck him on the left side of his chest with a laser-like focus. He considered that an omen. As he looked to his heart, he came to believe Colt had come into his life and *was* that tiny ray of light, piercing an otherwise impenetrable darkness—one that dwelt deep in his heart. The boy discovered the one small opening in a wall of doubt, depression and degradation he had built around himself. In time, the little man, single-handedly, brought down the entire wall. *Why do I want to run? Where would I go even if I got away? Do I have a future...of any kind...any place?* That small, highly focused beam of sunshine told him all he needed to know.

And then he heard voices. "I'll check back here," a man said. "Y'all go over there. Be careful! We don't know if he's armed or not." Pop almost decided to surrender, going so far as to reach for the plywood to shove it aside, but stopped short. He decided that, maybe, there was one last thing he needed to do first. Quietly and slowly he withdrew his hand and resumed his position on the dirt floor, accompanied by a long slow exhale. He waited. While he did, he hatched a plan.

When darkness set in and he could move about freely, he cautiously exited the old cellar and began a search for a telephone. The plan was to find people he had not talked to in twenty years or more.

TWENTY

Pop broke into an unoccupied home. Once he located it, he used the phone to make calls. He then left all the cash he carried, eighteen dollars and change, by the phone to cover the charges, plus a note of apology for the minor scarring damage around the door where he pried it open.

Afterwards, he saw no more reason to remain out of sight. He returned to the place it all began, the third story walk-up apartment over the jewelry store. It had been a long night. The walk to downtown Green Meadow took some time from where he was at the edge of town. When he arrived he sank down with a groan on the steps at the bottom of the narrow stairwell facing the sidewalk. Now, he could only wait for dawn and see what the light of day might bring. He was dirty, tired and sore, not too different than when he first came to town. But that was the only similarity. It was only physical. On the inside, he was a totally transformed individual. Through the night, with no place to go and nothing remaining to be done, he turned inward and relived a phenomenal year.

As he resurfaced from those thoughts, he noticed it becoming lighter. It was dawn. The eastern horizon had begun its spectacular daily metamorphosis. It went from dark indigo to lighter hues and finally an orange fingernail broke the horizon, exploding in color. Such beauty was worth a reverent look, although Pop realized the prudent thing would be to go immediately to the sheriff's office in the interest of safety—to himself and people on the street. Nonetheless, doing the prudent thing just did not seem all that important anymore.

Looking toward the diner, he saw farmers and townspeople streaming into it and reminisced about the day Colt appeared in front of him holding that cup. A fifty-cent cup of coffee was all it took to begin a journey he would repeat in a heartbeat, if given the opportunity.

Green Meadow was a small town. The only place the word *secret* existed was in a dictionary. In this community a secret had no more chance of survival than a wrinkle in the belly of Ledbetter's overalls or on one of Marge Bradshaw's finely made beds. Everyone not only knew one another, they also knew all the details of personal lives as well. By now, the entire town knew what had happened. The people he saw entering the diner were already deep in conversations about Ledbetter. It was a buzz of opinions and gossip, some true, but most took on lives of their own, embellished beyond good sense. One he clearly overheard was that he held a machete to Ledbetter's throat and made him beg for his life before slitting his throat. As outlandish as it was, this rumor came closer to the truth than most.

Main Street became busier by the minute. Stores on the square began to open, but Pop just sat, lost in thought until Raeford Willis arrived to open his jewelry store and did a double take, recognizing him. "Pop? Is that you?" Without looking up, the old man nodded.

"You do realize every law enforcement officer in the county is looking for you. Don't you?" Raeford asked then began backing away.

Pop did not answer, but did not appear unpleasant either, as he looked up to make eye contact with Raeford.

"You know, Burton Ledbetter was pretty darned worthless in most people's eyes around here," Raeford said in a bolder voice, "But you didn't have to kill him."

"I know," Pop said. Further commentary was pointless.

One by one, a small group of curious onlookers gathered. They talked among themselves but no one addressed Pop directly. They all just looked down at the dirty little old man sitting on the lower step beside the jewelry store forming a semi-circle around him. There was no anger or fear among them, just curious eyes.

Finally, Pop slapped his knee and said, "Well, I suppose it's time for me to go." The crowd parted when he stood, as though there was a quiet consensus among these law-abiding

144

Christian folks that he should leave town before the law caught up with him.

Pop made his way through the still-developing corridor of townsfolk unhurried. No one attempted to stop him. A few of them smiled as he walked by. The awkward quiet was finally broken by an elderly man leaning on his cane near the back of the crowd. "I think they ought to give him a goddamned medal," he yelled.

A train whistle split the air from the direction of the grain elevator at the end of Main Street. It was a signal the train was about to pull away. A woman cried, "Hurry up, Pop, you need to get on that train and don't look back. Please hurry and go."

The crowd became bolder. "If I'd been there," a man said gruffly, "I would have given you a gun to make it quicker and cleaner. Darn it all…there was no reason to get dirty over it." He punctuated by spitting on the sidewalk, as Pop walked by.

Making no response, Pop emerged from the crowd as two Department of Public Safety vehicles and the sheriff's car squealed to a stop on the street near him. The officers jumped out, drew their weapons and shouted, "Lie face down on the sidewalk, arms and legs spread! Do it now!"

One of the officers turned to the crowd and ordered them to back away. The crowd moved in unison like a receding tide.

Pop complied with their order and one of the officers holstered his gun and retrieved his handcuffs from a pouch on his belt. The young deputy was unnecessarily rough. He put a knee in the middle of Pop's back and yanked his arms behind him, then snapped the cuffs securely on the old man's wrists. The officer held him down on the cool concrete of the sidewalk while he read the Miranda Rights. The crowd inched in closer, as he did. Pop's cheek was still on the concrete but looked up to see a sad pair of eyes peering down at him. He recognized them as belonging to the old lady that ran the diner just down the street. He was then roughly lifted to his feet and placed in

145

the back seat of the sheriff's car. It had been specially outfitted with an expanded metal cage for carrying prisoners.

Pop sat dejected, his head hung limply from his shoulders. That mouthy old man wagged his cane at the back of the car he sat in and declared, "It's a shame. It's a goddamned shame, I tell ya. There's no justice if they convict that man." The sheriff's deputy cranked the car and sped away.

The sheriff's department and attached county jail was just off the square within sight of the courthouse. Pop was taken inside and officials methodically processed him in. He calmly did everything he was told. While a deputy took his fingerprints, a clerk in the adjoining office asked someone across the room, "Did you hear about that little Bradshaw boy?"

"What did you hear about him?" Pop demanded, snapping his head around, straining against the deputy to see into the next room.

A portly woman with her hair in a bun and a pencil protruding from it leaned in. "Word is, he passed away in his sleep last night," she said, "Leukemia took him quicker than anyone expected. I understand the family is in terrible shock. No wonder really. He was so young. The poor boy never really had a chance to know what life's all about."

"Let me tell you something," Pop said, "That boy knew *exactly* what life was all about. He had more knowledge of life, living and love in the tip of his little finger than most of us will possess in a lifetime."

**

The little white church with the top-heavy steeple overflowed. Cars were parked in the ditch along the road for hundreds of yards. Some even pulled their vehicles into the adjacent cotton field to park. Flower arrangements filled the front of the church and scented the warm air. Baskets and wreaths that did not fit inside were placed on either side of the front door.

High clouds streamed southward behind a front that created blustery north winds. Temperatures reflected the

146

approaching autumn and began to drop. The warm breeze transformed into cool gusty wind in a matter of seconds and picked up loose sand and debris, sending it scurrying southward in streams through the churchyard.

As Ella Minyard played Rock of Ages on the organ, the widow craned her neck to see Pop escorted down the center aisle of the crowded church in a county-issued orange jump suit, hands cuffed to his front and connected to a chain strung to shackles on his ankles. Every eye followed him. They all knew the story. Two deputies guided him to the open casket in front of the church.

Staring into the peaceful little face, he was awash with a lifetime of memories all made in a single year. He stood over his little friend, as long as he was allowed, then pulled away to a seat reserved next to the family. Because of Tom and Marge Bradshaw's standing in the community, their request to let Pop attend the service had been honored.

The procession to the cemetery consisted of an impressive string of vehicles over a quarter mile long. Most of the population of Bentley County attended the service and now snaked its way down a series of intersecting dirt roads. The community cemetery was isolated about five miles from the church and stood on a hillside far from the nearest farmhouse.

A tent had been set up by the funeral home and strained against its supports with each gust of wind. The somber group of family and closest friends sat tightly packed within the small space beneath it. Pop, with deputies on either side, stood at the back corner.

The preacher read two scriptures, said a short prayer, and then people filed by the family with individual condolences. Aside from wind, the only sounds were occasional sniffles and muffled whispers. The crowd gradually dwindled until all that remained were Tom, Marge, Pop and his guards.

After a time, the funeral home employees began dismantling the tent and folding the chairs.

The two parents stood by the casket and mourned the loss of their only child. It was clearly difficult to leave the tyke behind. With the approval of the deputies, Pop walked around

147

in front of them, his hands still cuffed. Marge turned her red swollen eyes upward to meet his. "Ma'am," Pop said, "I want you and Tom to know that that boy of yours was one of the finest human beings I've ever seen. It was a privilege to have been given the chance to know him. I'm not sure it's something I deserved, but I'll forever cherish having had the opportunity."

Tom threw a hefty arm around Pop's neck and squeezed. Then Marge hugged him long and hard. "Don't worry, Pop," she said, choking back tears, "we're going to work at making sure things turn out okay for you. We've contacted an attorney in Abilene that was recommended. There are many people in Green Meadow that care more than you know."

"Oh no, Ma'am." Pop said. "Don't do anything. Everything that needs doing, I've already taken care of." Tom and Marge looked at one another, confused. "Do you trust me?" Pop asked.

"Sure we do," Tom said.

"Then trust me on this. All I want you to do is harvest a good crop." And with that Pop walked away, deputies fell in behind.

The sobs of the grieving parents was underscored by the clank and hum of the electric wench lowering Colt into the ground, just as a strong north wind raked the cemetery on its way to sweep the Texas plains with its sorrow.

TWENTY ONE

It was late September. Pop's murder trial was about to get underway. Since he had only been a resident for about a year, no venue change was sought, though Judge William Breck was brought in from neighboring Bilton County. Orwen Blalock, the presiding Bentley County judge, excused himself after publicly espousing his personal opinion on the case, which was a not-too-well-disguised reference to Ledbetter being poorly equipped to be a member of the human race.

Several locals offered to pay the expense of good legal counsel for Pop. His reply to them all was the same as it was to the Bradshaws, "No, but thanks anyway."

At peace, Pop spent his time in confinement reading or conversing with the guards. He was confident everything would turn out just the way he intended.

Marge and Tom stopped by his cell almost every day to see if he needed anything or just sit and visit for a while. They kept him supplied with books, magazines and various forms of reading material. They attempted capitalizing on every opportunity to convince him he should fight for his freedom. But, after a smile and a thank you, Pop invariably changed the subject.

Lorraine Shumacher was Pop's court-appointed attorney. A nervous, highly skittish girl fresh from passing the bar exam, Lorraine was eager to get a legal career on track and test her legal wings. Though highly educated and well trained, it was a new venture for her. It kept her off-balance, but she had flashes of calm each time she realized self-defense would likely be the verdict. She could not see it going any other way. Her confidence grew that even should she falter, it still would not be enough to mess things up bad enough to prevent it. The outcome was that certain and she was not the only one to think so.

Pop liked her. At their first meeting, a rapid symbiotic chemistry between them made itself known. The meetings were usually lighthearted. So much so, Lorraine found it necessary to keep Pop focused on the business at hand. But, by his way of thinking, that business was hers, not his. Pop treated her in a fatherly way.

"Mr. Peterson—"

"I wish you'd stop calling me that."

"I'm sorry," she said, "But I need to remain accustomed to formally addressing you. So when we get into the courtroom—"

"Are you afraid the entire judicial system will fall into ruin if you call me Pop in open court?"

"Well, no…Pop," she stammered.

"That's a little better." The old man waved an emphatic, but friendly, finger at her then smiled. "Now, you practice saying the name until it rolls off naturally."

"Okay, Mr. Pet… uh, Pop. I feel like we can convince the jury that Burton Ledbetter's death was self defense…"

"Whatever," he said, "but ya know what I'd really like right now?"

"What?" she asked, her frustration climbing.

"Fried chicken," he said, licking his lips then smacking them, "cooked with a hint of sage and dusted with cayenne pepper."

Puzzled, "Pop, I don't understand your cavalier attitude. This is your way of life at stake here," she said. "For God's sake, don't you want this trial to end in your favor?"

"Oh, yes ma'am. I know exactly how this trial should end and I'll be sorely disappointed if it ends any other way."

While she continued to explain her planned defense, Pop sat back in his chair, fingers laced behind his head, and heard little of what his legal counsel had to say. But he *did* admire her zeal to hone her craft. As the days went by, he developed a deep respect for the girl. It bordered on affection.

**

There was a dry chill in the early autumn air. People set aside daily routines to get a good seat in the gallery at the courthouse. The hum of the cotton gin at the northern edge of Green Meadow was constant in the background as freshly picked cotton came in to it regularly now.

The aromatic, and not unpleasant, smell of burning cotton burrs wafted across town, a welcomed addition to the air in farm country, conjuring visions of a job well done, a paycheck coming, even the approach of the holidays.

Pop's trial garnered considerable interest, especially in the home county. Word-of-mouth brought in curious folks from a much wider area. Newspaper and television reporters from Lubbock and as far away as Wichita Falls picked up on the trial; hearing only that a transient had killed a local farmer in a fit of rage yet had no desire for exoneration. It piqued interest in those looking for stories with a fascinating slant.

The first day of testimony found the courtroom full. The prosecution presented its case first and attempted establishing a scenario of anger that turned deadly. Witnesses were presented that knew of, or had seen, tension between Pop and old man Ledbetter. The prosecution witnesses had obviously been coached by the district attorney's office. Even then, some could not help but say things incriminating about Burton Ledbetter. The prosecuting attorney had to work harder at hiding the truth than producing it.

Fidgeting with papers and taking notes while she sat, belied Lorraine's expertise each time she rose to engage witnesses. She kept a tissue handy to roll across her sweaty palms. Then, with the grace of a Shakespearean actor, she took on an admirable air of confidence, performing cross-examinations, not allowing testimony hinting anything other than self-defense. With two of those prosecution witnesses, she successfully turned potentially damaging testimony to a self-defense slant.

Not concerned in the slightest with the outcome of the trial, Pop's only interest in the proceedings was his defense counsel's performance. Silently, he cheered her on, hoping her

151

talents as a budding defense attorney would continue to blossom as they appeared to be doing. He doodled on a tablet. The business of the courtroom was only a drone on the fringes of consciousness. But there was no reason for impatience. He figured patience would be a handy thing to have as a survival skill in prison. He might as well become accustomed to it.

The prosecution rested mid-afternoon without making a strong case against the old man and proceedings, to this point, looked promising for Pop or, more specifically, for the defense. Once the prosecuting attorney formally rested, Judge Breck recessed until 9 o'clock the next morning.

It was assumed by almost everyone that the defense would present its case, the trial would go to the jury by lunchtime on the second day, and a verdict of self-defense would be returned, all within a short period. The collective opinion by all Bentley County residents following details of the trial seemed to lean toward total exoneration and release, even among those who were aware Pop had no desire to be released.

The second day of the trial began. Reporters who had come hoping for something more sensational began to agree with the prediction of self-defense and took to loitering in the hall outside the courtroom, disinterested but obligated to see it through to conclusion.

Entering the courtroom, Lorraine was the picture of confidence, producing a series of witnesses that included Tom and Marge. In turn, they testified that Ledbetter had threatened Pop.

As the prosecution cross-examined the last of the defense witnesses, Pop leaned into Lorraine and whispered, "It's time."

She snapped her head back, confused. "Time for what?"

"Time you put me on the stand."

Only with great effort could she keep her voice down. "What do you mean it's 'time to put *you* on the stand'?" she said in a harsh whisper. "That's a terrible idea. Things are going good, just as they are. Believe me, Pop, this is not the time to be experimenting."

"Yes, things *are* going good and, you're doing a magnificent job," he said squeezing her hand, "But experimentation is the farthest thing from my mind."

"Now, tell the court you're calling, as your next witness, Paul Odell Peterson, a.k.a. Pop to the stand. Or, I'll request you be dismissed as my legal counsel," he said in the calm manner of a stern disciplinarian.

Lorraine stared at him dumbstruck. Slack-jawed, she slowly shook her head. She did not hear the judge's repeated instructions to call her next witness. She knew what needed to be said and she knew what needed to be done but, suddenly, she could not do any of it. That look of confusion shifted to the judge.

An awkward silence filled the courtroom. "Does the defense have any further witnesses?" the judge repeated impatiently.

"Yes, Your Honor, at his request and against counsel's advice," she said, looking back into Pop's eyes, "I'm calling Paul Odell Peterson, a.k.a. Pop to the stand."

A hum of whispers rose from the gallery. The judge rapped his gavel and ordered, "Quiet!" Looking across the sea of faces until silence had been restored. Those outside the courtroom, having heard the commotion, crowded around the door.

Pop strode to the witness stand sporting a relaxed and pleasant look, appearing as a man casually strolling down a shady sidewalk on a sunny spring Sunday afternoon. He raised his right hand upon request and was sworn in, "Do you swear to tell the truth, the whole truth and nothing but the truth, so help you God?"

"I most certainly do," Pop said loudly, his back straight. "The only time I've ever lied was to protect the innocent."

Again the gallery became disruptive, this time with laughter. Judge Breck rapped the gavel hard and pointed it at the noisiest offenders, threatening to have them ejected.

Silence finally returned and the judge admonished Pop for his flippancy, ordering the swearing-in to be repeated. The second time, Pop simply answered with a smile, "Yes. I do."

Lorraine took considerable time to approach the witness stand. It was apparent she was tense, not certain what the old man had on his mind. But, she had no choice and began. "Mr. Peterson..." She cast a knowing grin in response to his smile and began again. "May I call you Pop?" she asked.

"Please do."

"Pop, could you describe for the court the events that led to Burton Ledbetter's death, as you know them to be?"

Pop looked toward the floor for a moment to collect his thoughts then to the judge. "Your Honor," he said then looked to the jury box, "ladies and gentlemen of the jury, I feel that it's my responsibility to tell you exactly what happened that day behind the feed store..."

Lorraine backed away, standing beside the defense table, nervously drumming her fingers on it.

"...After I left Colt Bradshaw's room at the hospital, I attempted to clear my mind by walking. I had no destination in mind and the reason for me being behind that feed store at the exact time Burton Ledbetter was loading his pickup truck was purely coincidental."

The gallery grew quiet and Lorraine relaxed a bit. "Had I thought about killing Ledbetter at any time before that day? Oh, I most certainly had, on several occasions." Lorraine frowned offering a quick but subtle headshake, not liking the direction he seemed to be taking.

"The first time," he continued, "was when his oldest son accosted six-year old Colt Bradshaw in a theatre restroom and then pulled a knife on me when I tried to intervene." He scanned the faces of the jurors. "I thought whoever that boy's father was needed killing. I didn't even know who Burton Ledbetter was at that time." Snickers went up from random spectators near the rear of the gallery.

"Not long after that incident, Burton Ledbetter himself drunkenly attacked me in the restroom of the high school the night of the winter carnival. He displayed a callous arrogance by including six-year old Colt Bradshaw in the fray, recklessly endangering his safety, not just mine." A flush of anger reddened his face. He took a deep breath, adding more calmly,

154

"Again, the thought crossed my mind that that man needed killing. But, I showed *considerable* restraint by only knocking him unconscious."

Once again, snickers and muffled laughter was scattered throughout the room, this time accompanied by a general buzz of unintelligible conversation. Judge Breck rapped his gavel. "I'll clear this gallery if you can't keep it quiet," he again threatened then paused. "And I'm serious about that." He paused again. "Please continue Mr. Peterson."

Reporters pulled out notepads and recorders. The trial, quite suddenly, had taken an interesting turn. "The next time I encountered Burton Ledbetter," Pop said, "was at his own daughter's funeral. There, he blatantly displayed a lack of remorse or even an ounce of love for that precious little girl. After the funeral service at the church, that poor excuse for a human being displayed an audacious arrogance by verbally attacking me, and the Bradshaws, as being responsible for the child's death. And, guess what?" A few heads nodded. Pop raised his voice to a new level. "That's right. You guessed it. I thought he needed killing."

Judge Breck admonished Pop for his derogatory reference to the deceased. "My apology to the court, Your Honor," he said. "That day, though, in the alley behind the feed store, I had no intention of so much as speaking to the man. My mind was on matters infinitely more important, but a few ill-timed and crude comments from Ledbetter changed all that." Pop stiffened his back and declared, "At that moment I could think of no one on the face of this planet who needed killing more than a big, stinking farmer by the name of Burton Ledbetter." His voiced crescendo into a high-pitched exclamation, "and I thought I was just the person to get it done!"

The courtroom exploded in gasps of disbelief. "I object!" Lorraine said, almost shouting.

"You shouldn't be able to, since he's your witness and your client, Judge Breck said over the buzz and rap of his own gavel, "But I'm inclined to sustain it anyway."

The large oak double-doors squeaked open a crack and several faces stacked in the narrow opening as curious people peered into the courtroom. Raising his voice to be heard above the din and echo of the still rapping gavel, Pop disregarded the sustained objection. "There are two absolutely indisputable facts, he said, now nearly shouting, "I thought about killing him...I had planned to kill him...and when I found the opportunity, I did!"

Lorraine yelled above the roar in the room, "Your Honor, please..." The noise in the courtroom made it nearly impossible for any single voice to be heard.

"No one, and I do mean *no one*, needed removing from the human race more than Burton Ledbetter!" Pop shouted.

"I want to see counsel in my chambers immediately," the judge said, still rapping his gavel. "There'll be a ten minute recess."

The bailiff approached the stand and escorted Pop from the courtroom. Lorraine and the prosecuting attorney followed the black-robed judge through the door behind the bench. No one in the courtroom moved. There was suddenly ample reason to stay until the end. The drama was far from over. In fact, it had just begun.

As soon as the heavy door of the judges' chamber closed behind them, Lorraine started to speak but the judge stopped her. He held a hand up then gestured her toward a chair. She sat. "Ms. Schumacher, do you realize what you've done by allowing your client to take the stand? Do you understand that your client has taken what, most probably would have been, a verdict of self-defense," the judge told her, "And turned it into a confession of murder, carrying much greater consequences?"

Dejected, head hung low, Lorraine raised her eyes to meet the judge's. "Yes, Your Honor," she said, "but you have to understand—".

"In your opinion, is your client of sound mind?"

Lorraine hesitated then frowned. It was clear she did not know what to do. "Yes. I believe he is. But there's—"

"Then the court has no choice but to accept the defendant's admission and have it entered into the official court record," Judge Breck said in a much lower, somber tone.

The recess ended. Players returned to the courtroom. Lorraine could not take her eyes away from Pop. Even if what he said were true, it certainly was not the whole story. Try as she might to prepare her final argument to the jury, Lorraine had great difficulty setting aside the confusing swirl of questions. She struggled to focus on her last chance to convince the jury it was indeed self-defense, regardless of the defendant's comments on the witness stand and obvious lack of concern for his own freedom.

Realizing she was confused, Pop patted her hand. "This is the way it's supposed to go," he said. This is the way I want it to go."

Clenching her teeth with renewed determination, she whispered, "It may be the way *you* want it to go, but I'll be damned if I let you do this to yourself."

Pop felt a chilled breeze upon hearing Lorraine's determined comment, which was impossible in the stuffy, windowless courtroom. "Colt?" he mumbled.

"Does the defense have any further witnesses?" the judge asked.

"Your Honor," Lorraine said, as she faced the bench, "In light of today's events, I respectfully request a twenty-four continuance." Receiving no objections from the prosecution, Judge Breck granted the request and announced court would reconvene in two days at 9 a. m.

The courtroom cleared rapidly. Echoes of many voices died away. Lorraine had been staring at Pop, and finally asked, "Why?"

"You're a fine attorney and have a brilliant future ahead of you," Pop said. He hugged her. He then pecked her on the cheek as the bailiff took his arm and, more gently than is customary, pulled him away.

"You may have given up on yourself," she said to his back, "But I'm not ready to give up on you."

157

"No. Don't do anything that will prolong this," he said over his shoulder. "Do you understand?"

"No, damn it, I don't understand!" she said, standing straight and defiant. Then let her head fall. "I don't understand you at all."

Again, a tiny but unmistakable chilled breath brushed Pop's cheek as he and the bailiff disappeared through the door.

TWENTY TWO

The springs of the narrow iron bed squawked under his weight as Pop repositioned, placing his back against the wall it set against, knees drawn to his chest. He rested his chin on two stacked fists atop his knees. The environment of his cell, stark and uninviting to most, happened to be the perfect atmosphere at the moment for his purpose. He allowed his mind to drift over sixty-three years of life. Although unintended, he reassessed all he had been through, all he had endured, and tried to judge it against some measuring stick. The memories ran the gamut, some dark, some happy, but all remembered from the same reference point, a near perfect year living on the Bradshaw farm with Colt at his side. The measuring device he settled on was that year. All others paled. Everything he remembered prior to it seemed to have been aimed in that direction. All tragedies and triumphs, seen in retrospect, now appeared to have been purposeful, driving him toward a young boy at a prescribed point in the future, two lives destined to meld. Now all arrows pointed backwards to the year just ended. The center of his universe died and set him adrift.

Recently, on several occasions, he started to explain to Tom and Marge—even his attorney, Lorraine—why he felt that to end his freedom was not a tragic scenario, preferring, as he did, to believe it a fitting punctuation to a wonderful year. He could not imagine returning to a life of mere existence. There was no hesitation. He realized, beyond all doubt, life could never be better, or even equal to, the previous year—anywhere, anytime, under any circumstances. It was the best way out of Green Meadow, courtesy of the Texas legal system. Trying to explain was pointless, knowing, as he did, that forward-looking people, as they were, would refuse to understand and try to dissuade his decision. Nonetheless, he knew many people struggled on his behalf for a favorable verdict—a verdict he did not consider favorable or desirous.

He shuddered to think what might become of him, should they succeed in having him freed. Left unstructured, his life would surely drift back to a new bottle of gin and another bottle of pills as his companions. He had not planned for that, and did all he could do to prevent it. He wanted to thank the community, not be a burden on it. He wanted to reward Tom and Marge for their kindness and the wonderful experience that would have been impossible without their blessings and support. More importantly, he wanted to let them know, in specific terms, the blessing Colt Bradshaw had been. Taking care of things he deemed necessary had been set in motion by a telephone call to Chicago the night before his arrest. It was a comfort to know this would be done once he was out of the picture.

The Bentley County Jail was never totally quiet, even late into the night. But, Pop became accustomed to the constant clanging echoes of metal on metal. *If it's this noisy in a small county jail, it's unimaginable that I'll ever get any sleep at the penitentiary in Huntsville.* An unintelligible human voice wailed from within the row of jail cells, shattering his thoughts. *Just another nightmare, perhaps. Bad dreams are common here.*

Stone and steel did not allow the heating system to do its job properly and a strong, late-September wind chilled his cell, which was against a northerly facing wall. Pop shivered and pulled his knees in tighter.

By his reckoning, he was blessed. He had come so close, so many times to taking his own life. Each time, some indescribable force stepped in to ease the overpowering inclination to end it all. Each time it did, it was an unsettling and baffling feeling he never reconciled. Now, he saw it as just one more guidepost that pushed him towards the Bradshaw family. Pop held no particular religious belief system but had come to suspect the existence of a higher power, if for no other reason than *only* a supreme being could have produced Colt Bradshaw then introduce the lad into his life at such a pivotal point; a small child who just happened to think it was a good idea to bring him a cup of coffee. From that day, the old man began a transformation. His view of the world would never be the same again. "I suppose there could be a god out there…somewhere," he muttered, looking up to the roughly texture concrete ceiling. *God? A supreme being? An unseen ruler of the universe? Maybe.* He still had trouble believing. But, now, he wondered.

The events of the previous year were simply too fantastic to be cast aside as a random cosmic accident. Why, inexplicably, had he not committed suicide long ago? Why had he not taken those pills and washed them down with that pint of gin during one of those many bouts of depression? It would have been so easy and painless. *Did some power beyond my comprehension mean for me to spend that year and absorb the wisdom of an innocent child? Had some deity declared that lessons were yet to be learned? Or, maybe, that I should know love again before my time on earth was finished?*

The clack, clack of hard heels on concrete stopped at his cell and snapped him back to the moment. "Is everything okay, Pop," a uniformed man said through the bars. "You should be asleep."

The old man looked up into the eyes of a young deputy. He smiled and nodded. "Just travelin' a road paved with memories, son. That's all." The deputy smiled, tapped the bars with his stick and walked on.

Pop's eyes settled on the pale light through a very small high window, beyond where the deputy had stood. The view of the moon was distorted through the thick, reinforced glass, but the silvery light took him back to one special evening when a full moon had served as a hard lesson on the importance of tradition. At the time he believed he was teaching the lesson, but the reality was, as he now knew it, he was the recipient of it. He was the student, Colt Bradshaw the teacher.

"Colt," he began, eyes fixed on the glow from the window, "I don't know if there is a god or not, but, the way I see it, if there is one, he'd probably listen to you before he would me. I let evil thoughts dictate an idle life and wasted most of it out of self-pity. But you, boy, were pure." Pop chewed the inside of his cheek, feeling vaguely embarrassed he

161

might be overheard, sneaking a glance through the bars of his cell for movement. Seeing none, he shook it off. "I have a simple request I'd like for you to pass along to the Big Kahuna," he said. "Could you do that for me, boy?"

He felt a small chill that was, somehow, different. He took it as a yes. "I know how long the dictionary says eternity is and I'm hoping it's just as long up there, and, if it's okay with the Boss, I'd just as soon spend it with you, when the time comes." Pop suddenly felt very comfortable, as if a weight had been lifted. He became drowsy. "I think I might have to hang around down here a while longer, though." He yawned.

Feeling his eyelids becoming heavy, Pop succumbed to the exhaustive events of the day and lay down. As he began drifting into a twilight sleep, he muttered, "And see if it would be okay if Jane Ledbetter could join us. She's a good kid. I think the three of us will have a grand time together."

TWENTY THREE

Less than two days was all it took for the rapidly changing Texas weather to transform the appearance of the people crowding into the courtroom, from short sleeves and perspiration to heavy jackets and red noses. North wind, racing down from Canada, pushed people about on the street with ease.

Judging by the standing-room-only crowd, a cold windy day would not be enough to keep people away from the courthouse. They came and kept coming. Folks in this part of the state seldom had the opportunity to witness such a strange legal turn of events. Most had a vaulted curiosity and calendars were cleared to make time to attend. Disagreements and debate flared like sporadic wildfires on the eventual outcome. The diner on the corner was the scene of a near-brawl when groups with opposing opinions almost got out of hand the day before. They all wanted to know firsthand how the old man's story would end. Gambling was frowned on around the conservative town of Green Meadow. But it was no secret that bets were made on how the jury would vote, given the incriminating testimony by Pop at the last session. The trial was the number one topic of conversation, but not only around Green Meadow and Bentley County, but over a much wider area thanks to the media picking up the story.

Unbeknownst to Pop, he had become a local celebrity. The name Paul Odell Peterson and the nickname, Pop, was suddenly widely recognized and part of every conversation. Reporters from television, radio, and newspapers from as far away as Dallas and Austin came to cover the trial. Smaller market media from Abilene, Wichita Falls and Lubbock had been here all along. Everyone wanted an interview with the enigmatic old man that would rather go to prison than be freed. Pop refused every attempt at being interviewed. He did not view it as worth talking about. Video cameras were set up in a crowded corner at the rear of the room. Men and women with audio recorders, note pads and 35-millimeter cameras stood ready to record the proceedings.

Escorting Pop into the courtroom from a side door, the bailiff walked the old man to his assigned chair next to Ms. Schumacher. Pop craned his neck, curiously studying the noisy gallery. People clamored for even a square foot of floor space to stand. As he sat, "Lorraine, what's with the packed house?"

"It was that ill-timed and crazy little speech you gave on the witness stand day before yesterday," Lorraine told him. "You may not have intended for it to happen this way, but you've captured the interest and imagination of a lot of people." She tried to look serious but even as she shook her head, a smile almost formed.

Everyone in the courtroom stood as the bailiff announced the entrance of Judge William Breck to the bench. Court was officially in session. "Ms. Schumacher," Judge Breck asked, "Are you ready to resume with your defense of the accused?"

"Yes, Your Honor. I am," she replied as she rose. She leaned down and cupped her hand around Pop's ear. "And, so help me," she whispered, "If you make so much as a peep, I'll ask the judge to have you removed from this courtroom." He smiled and winked up at her.

No smile this time. She was all business with a clenched jaw. "Your Honor," she began, "During the last session we called witnesses that addressed Burton Ledbetter's threats against Mr. Peterson and other derogatory comments that were made about my client by the deceased. Today, with the court's indulgence, I *will* show that Paul Odell Peterson has become much more than just a transient passing through Green Meadow."

With a wrinkle of curiosity, Pop watched as his young attorney took control—total control. "If I could ask the bailiff to escort them in," Lorraine told the court, "I have assembled a few people willing to vouch for Mr. Peterson's character."

Pop turned to watch the doors behind them, and so did every other head in the courtroom. The double doors swung open and leading the way into the room were Tom and Marge

Bradshaw, followed by the Bradshaw's neighbor, Bud Landry, Tom's friend Bobby Joe Peeler, the widow Ella Minyard, Raeford Willis from the jewelry store, Doctor Howard Tidwell, Deputy Barry Brown and the entire staff of the emergency room at Bentley County Hospital who had been on duty the morning of Marge's heart attack when he brought her in for treatment.

But, the parade of folks did not stop with them; also coming through the door was almost everyone that Pop had come in contact with during the previous year, people he barely knew—people whose lives he touched somehow and hadn't realized his effect on them.

The string of people astonished the old man, not having understood the impact he had had on people. He had trouble believing most of them would even remember him. That was a poor assumption.

Lorraine met his look of astonishment with a confident wink of her own. She began calling witnesses. It took over an hour for all the stories to be told and the prosecution could do very little to discredit any of them. The final witness was Doctor Howard Tidwell, the Bradshaw's family physician. Doctor Tidwell," Lorraine asked, "what has been your association with the defendant?"

"Very little. I barely know the man."

"Then why have you chosen to be here today on his behalf?"

"Because," the doctor said, pointing to Marge Bradshaw," That woman, right there, might very well not be alive and sitting in this courtroom today had it not been for the heroic effort of Mr. Peterson. I certainly believe that someone who'd fight as hard as he did to save a life would not purposely kill anyone, and certainly not murder them." Wide-eyed, tears welling, Pop sat, awash with emotion, and listened. The prosecution had no questions for the doctor and Lorraine rested the case for the defense.

Then came final arguments. Lorraine gave a lengthy summation and then wrapped it up. "...And *that*, ladies and gentlemen of the jury is why the defense contends it is patently *absurd* that Paul Odell Peterson murdered Burton Ledbetter. I beseech you to render the *only* logical verdict and that is acquittal by reason of self-defense." She walked the length of the jury box silently and then ended with, "Thank you." She then took the time to make eye contact with all twelve, one at a time, before returning to her seat.

Judge Breck began his instructions to the jury. "Ladies and gentleman of the jury, though the damaging testimony of the accused is a matter of record, the evidence does not support the gravity of his comments. Therefore I urge you to temper your decision with, not only, the hard evidence presented, but also by the testimony you've heard today." The judge went on to explain the choices of verdicts, and punishment ranges for each, before dismissing them to a sealed room for deliberations.

The packed courtroom cleared grudgingly. No one knew how long the jury would be out but no one wanted to possibly give up precious gallery space. Most wanted to hear the verdict as it was read. No one wanted to lose their seat, if they were lucky enough to have one to begin with. Even those that did see fit to go outside the courtroom to smoke or get something to eat did not venture far. The crowd milling about the courthouse waited impatiently for the jury to come back, and could have easily been mistaken for an audience to an outdoor concert or a speech by an important politician. A large number remained in a tight group near the door. By most people's reckoning, the trial was an event worthy of note because nothing like it had ever happened in Green Meadow before.

Less than two hours passed when the jury was escorted back into the courtroom. People pushed and shoved in to watch the verdict read. Court reconvened and Judge Breck had to quiet the gallery. All sound died away. Judge Breck asked, "Ladies and gentlemen of the jury, have you reached a verdict?"

"Yes, Your Honor. We have," said the jury foreman, handing a slip of paper to the bailiff who, then, handed it over to the judge.

Reading the slip with a frown, Judge Breck dropped his glasses onto a pile of papers in front of him and handed it back to the bailiff. "What's your verdict?" he asked the jury.

"We, the jury," said the foreman, as the bailiff returned the slip of paper to him, "find Paul Odell Peterson, also known as Pop, guilty of murder with passion and recommend five years in the state penitentiary in Huntsville with the possibility of parole after serving two years." The many voices of the crowd rocked the courtroom, in disbelief at the severity of the verdict.

Quietly, Pop listened without expression, staring straight ahead. Not so with Lorraine. She cringed with gritted teeth in absolute surprise that the jury would come back with such a harsh decision, having been confident of leniency, even total exoneration.

"We'll recess until 9 a. m. tomorrow, at which time formal sentencing will be handed down," Judge Breck said then rapped his gavel. He immediately disappeared through the door behind the bench.

Having heard what they came to hear, the crowded courtroom cleared quickly. Pop was led away. The cavernous chamber was now empty, save for Lorraine. She sat fuming. She rapidly tapped a pen atop the table in front of her, unwilling to let it go, unwilling to let it stand. Teeth still clenched and now grinding she pondered her options. The young attorney was angered that circumstances prevented her from a favorable verdict on her first criminal defense. She exploded and threw the pen toward the jury box. Slamming her hand on the table, it reverberated as she spoke to the empty judge's chair. "This is totally unacceptable and I'm not through with this yet!"

TWENTY FOUR

The tractor rolled along at a steady three miles per hour pace. A variety of birds hovered and swooped over freshly plowed ground that emerged from beneath the points, rolling soil away from the furrows. They all chirped and battled over the tastiest of worms and insects turned up in the fertile, damp earth.

Small dust clouds rose lazily from the plows, as they split the drier surface crust. The engine of the tractor droned at a constant rate. Tom held the big machine on the mark, scratched in the earth by the long-arm markers from the previous pass that guided his inside front wheel to mate the rows perfectly. It ensured each plowed pass was just as straight as the one before.

The early spring day was sunny and calm. Colorful wildflowers had begun to bloom in the ditches at the end of the rows, but Tom's mind was not on the weather, the day, or the wildflowers. His thoughts were held hostage by events of the previous year and his actions, that day, were merely perfunctory. He had so many questions and precious few answers. He knew that time would be the only thing to heal the raw wound of loss that left a gaping chasm in who he was. This was not the time.

Tom plowed several hundred yards from the house when he noticed the dust boiling skyward from beneath an approaching car. He watched it turn onto the tree-shaded lane that was the long driveway of their home.

**

Colt's bedroom was a constant, sad reminder. Because of this, Marge collected a few mementos. Otherwise, she, systematically, cleared his bedroom of all furnishings, toys and clothes. She'd sold the furniture, but almost everything else had been given to charity. The room was bare. The only thing left in it was memories, steeped into the walls, and those would never go away. Marge was not trying to hide or suppress Colt's memory. He would always be locked away in her heart. But she took a pragmatic approach to dealing with his death. Making herself busy had always been her way in stressful or troubling situations. She purposely stayed busy every day to work herself until exhausted. That way sleep came a little easier come nightfall. If she wallowed in sadness all day there would be no rest.

The very last item in his bedroom was a small rug just inside the bedroom door. She picked it up and headed for the backyard to beat the dust out of it before rolling it up for storage. As she came out into the yard, she saw Tom driving the tractor up to the house, presumably for lunch, though it was a bit early. About the same time, an approaching car caught her eye and it pulled to a stop at the side of the house.

Draping the rug over a low fence bordering the yard, Marge watched a pleasant looking, middle-aged man get out of the car, as Tom killed the engine on the tractor and stepped off it to join her.

"Good morning folks," he said affably, clutching a briefcase, "Are you the Bradshaws?"

Tom caught up to Marge, who approached the stranger. He put an arm around her waist then extended a friendly hand. "Yes, I'm Tom Bradshaw and this is my wife, Marge."

The stranger met Tom's hand with his own. "My name is Montford Glenn. But, please, call me Monty."

Marge cut an inquisitive glance at Tom. He took her cue. "Okay, Monty Glenn, what is it we can do for you?" he asked.

"It probably would be best if I explained the whole story before I broached the specific reason I'm here. It may take a few minutes. Is there someplace we might sit down and discuss it?"

Marge, a little confused, but always the perfect hostess said, "Well, all right. Why don't we go inside? We can be comfortable there. I'll fix some iced tea and we'll listen to your

170

story. How's that?" She looked to Tom then to Mr. Glenn and received no implied resistance to the idea.

On the way up the back hall toward the kitchen, she glimpsed Monty noticing then examining the montage of photographs on a cluttered bulletin board. Three of those photographs were of Colt, totally bald, and laughing. In all three snapshots, the youngster was pointing to, or touching, the bald head of Pop dressed in his work clothes. "Well, I'll be darned, if it isn't Paul," he said, leaning in to get a closer look, then moved on to catch up.

The three sat at the kitchen table. "Okay, if you wanted to arouse curiosity in two people, you've succeeded," Tom said, "Let's hear your story." Marge covered his hand with hers. "By the way," he added, "If you're trying to sell something, you're out of luck, if it costs more than a few cents. It has been a tough year around here."

"Mr. Bradshaw, I wouldn't know how to sell a fur coat to an Eskimo." Monty said, taking a long, slow drink of iced tea. "So, you certainly don't have to worry about getting a sales pitch...not from me anyway." He took another drink. "Man, I didn't know iced tea could taste so good." He smacked his lips. The smiling stranger laced his fingers together atop his briefcase. "Okay, here goes. Over twenty three years ago I worked part-time at a brokerage firm in a suburb of Chicago under the tutelage of Paul Peterson, while I was in law school..."

"Pop?" Tom asked.

"That's right. I've only recently discovered that *Pop* is the name he's going by. He had always been Paul, or Mister Peterson, to me." He paused. "Paul was my mentor and helped me tremendously when I was in law school and, thanks to him, I did eventually get my degree, passed the bar and set up my own practice. Believe me, I could go on for some time talking about how I wouldn't be where I am without his support and help at that time. But I don't want to bore you with details from, and about, a man you've just met. I only mention these things to establish my connection so you'll have a point of reference." Monty paused to see if the two might have questions.

171

Marge and Tom sat quiet and attentive. "I hadn't spoken to Paul since the fiasco that caused him to lose his job at the firm," he said, "I didn't even know he was still alive. Once I'd become aware of the whole story surrounding his dismissal, I couldn't help but assume the worst, that he was dead. The talk bandied about was that it had been suicide. But, no body was ever found. He was terribly despondent at the time. I really didn't know what to think. Then, late one night last autumn, I was awakened from a sound sleep by a phone call. Of course I didn't recognize the voice and refused to believe it was Paul."

"What made you believe him?" Marge asked.

"Well," he sighed, "the man just knew too many things about our relationship...things that only Paul would know."

"Okay, you've established for us a relationship with Pop," Tom said with a touch of cynicism, "That still doesn't even hint at why you're here."

"I'm getting to it, but you need this background to legitimize my reason for coming all the way from Chicago to Texas. Otherwise, I'm afraid you're simply not going to grasp, or even remotely believe, what I have to say," he said then looked down at the tabletop for a second. "You may have trouble believing it anyway...*even with* the explanation," he quickly added.

Marge and Tom leaned forward with renewed interest. "Give it a shot," Tom said, "We're listenin'."

"Well," Monty continued, "when Paul lost his immediate family, then his career, he became increasingly detached from friends, other family members and then, finally, disappeared altogether; like I said, I thought suicide, but I outwardly maintained that he was just missing. His siblings and parents, still alive at the time, managed to get control of his substantial estate. Through legal connivance, they had his estate liquidated and split the proceeds. The only thing that remained untouched was a safe deposit box and that was only because they were unaware of it. I was the only one who knew about it.

When Paul called that night, he asked me if it possibly remained untouched. I told him it did. It was a personal gesture on my part for all he'd done for me. I maintained the rent on it thinking, hoping, a definitive word on what happened to him would come out eventually. As I sit here telling you all this, I have no idea how long I would have kept it up. Thankfully, that's now a moot point. Paul didn't even want to know the exact contents. He just remembered there were a few stock certificates, insurance policies, pictures and other personal items, but he couldn't care less about specifics. He just knew it was the only thing left in this world that was his and hoped their might be something of value in it that he could pass on to you, because, as he told me that night, he was terribly uncertain about his future and wanted it taken care of then, because he might not have another chance."

A slamming screen door caused Monty to abruptly stop talking. Appearing around the corner, was Pop. "Thanks for coming all this way," he told Monty, "It means a lot to me." He held out a friendly hand as he approached.

With an ear-to-ear grin, Monty leaped up, grabbed the old man's hand and pulled him into a bear hug. "It wasn't all just for this piece of business," Monty said, "It's been a very long time. I thought it would be worth the trip just to see you." He quickly embraced Pop again, jovially slapping him on the back, almost giddy. "Damn, man, it's good to see you." He slapped Pop on the back a couple more times.

Pop returned the back pats then pushed Monty away.

He wagged a finger at Pop. "You have to explain your punishment to me again, Paul," Monty said, as he returned to his seat, "That has to be one of the most unorthodoxed and bizarre sentences I've ever heard of for a conviction of murder...of any type. I want to hear it again, just because it is so difficult to believe."

"Yep. Only in Bentley County, Texas could such a thing happen," Pop said, "But it's true. Judge Breck sentenced me to five years with no parole. But it wasn't at the penitentiary in Huntsville, where I expected it to be. I was remanded to the custodial care of Tom and Marge Bradshaw for

173

no less than five years and ordered to work out my time on the farm. I can't leave without supervision. But that's okay. I have nowhere to go."

"And it'll be five years of *hard* labor," Tom joked. "I guarantee you that."

"Pop," Marge asked, "What is all this about? What's Mr. Glenn doing here?"

"Why don't we just let Monty earn his fee and finish explaining it," Pop said. "When all this was prepared, I certainly had no expectations of being around to explain it myself anyway."

"In that case," Monty said, "I'll read the letter Pop intended for me to read to you in his absence, on this occasion."

Pop became visibly nervous. "I know what it says. I'll be getting back to work now." Pop quickly left the house and returned to his chores.

Producing an envelope from a sleeve in his briefcase, Monty ripped the end of it off, slid out the single sheet and slapped it open, smoothing it over the checkered tablecloth . He then read aloud, "*Folks, there are no words, I can think of, that adequately express my deep feelings for the Bradshaw family. The items you are given today, in no way, can replace the ready-acceptance and trust that was unselfishly lavished upon me. These are only things, mere tokens, given in humble appreciation for allowing me a year that renewed me and made me complete. Maybe there is something here that will help when the crop is poor. Forever grateful –Pop'*"

Marge threaded her arm through Tom's and leaned her head on his shoulder. Tom squeezed her hand. Monty took a flat cardboard box from his briefcase of the type stationery comes in and removed the lid. "In this box is the entire contents of that safe deposit box," he said, taking out a photograph of a man, fortyish, posing with a woman and two pre-teen girls. The man only vaguely resembled Pop. He was neatly dressed in a three-piece suit, his hair thick and dark and sported a beaming smile. The family was standing near a car that appeared to be parked about half way around a circular driveway, in front of a two-story house, all the trappings of wealth plainly visible.

Next, Monty pulled out a small pile of papers and waved them off-handedly saying, "You can keep these, or not. They have no value, only old insurance policies, long expired, but I am legally bound by my promise to Paul to explain all the contents and give you everything." Monty laced his fingers together, once again, on top of the table, waiting for any possible questions or comments. Receiving none, "Now, we're getting to the interesting part."

He paused for effect then turned the box bottom-side up. Out fell a pile of certificates about an inch high. "Mr. And Mrs. Bradshaw, what you are looking at are stock certificates to four separate businesses that, today, are all highly prosperous. All have undergone numerous splits and many years of appreciation. The oldest of the four stocks was purchased twenty-eight years ago. As of the close of trading on the stock exchange yesterday," he said, "unfolding a scrap of paper with a number scrawled on it, "These certificates had a cash value of nearly two million dollars."

As Tom and Marge sat in shock, Monty finished by saying, "It's now legally yours...*every dime.*"

**

Over the following weeks Pop avoided Tom and Marge. When he could not, he turned back every attempt to return the valuable certificates. The old man finally convinced them to buy additional land and expand their farming operation. "I really think you should, particularly since you have free labor for the next five years," he told them. They reluctantly agreed to the arrangement, but only if he allowed them to share ownership interest in the additional land with him.

Days came and went. Pop fell into a pattern of peaceful existence—a lifestyle he embraced. Although memories remained of all those dreadful years living on the streets of Chicago, they seemed more and more like a bad dream that he could no longer swear had actually happened.

One clear night in April, Pop finished feeding the livestock a bit later than usual. As he hung an empty bucket on a high nail, he stopped to admire a full moon set among bright stars in a clear sky. The air was comfortably cool and filled with the heady aroma of freshly cut alfalfa hay. The moment and the sight of that moon filled his head with wonderful memories.

As he dwelt on fond remembrances, he removed his gloves and climbed atop the corner post of the corral. He was belted with a strong sense of déjà vu the second his butt hit the top of that post, remembering a small boy struggling to drag a heavy bale of hay toward him as he sat atop this same post once before. All, because that boy believed deeply in what he was doing.

Shifting his gaze to the full moon, "Colt you never gave up on me, did ya, boy? Even in death, I felt you at the trial. You weren't about to let Lorraine just let it go, were ya?" He climbed down from his perch and dusted his pants off. "Our day will come, boy. Our day will most assuredly come. Pleasant dreams and sleep tight. Good night Mr. Moon…good night."

THE END

"I wanted a perfect ending. …Now I've learned, the hard way, that some poems don't rhyme and some stories don't have a clear beginning, middle and end. Life is about not knowing, having to change, taking the moment and making the best of it, without knowing what's going to happen next. Delicious ambiguity." –Gilda Radner, American comedienne, 1946-1989